A MADE IN JERSEY NOVEL

# CRASHED
## Out

A MADE IN JERSEY NOVEL

# CRASHED
*Out*

# TESSA BAILEY

Entangled Publishing, LLC
2614 South Timberline Road
Suite 105, PMB 159
Fort Collins, CO 80525
rights@entangledpublishing.com

Brazen is an imprint of Entangled Publishing, LLC.

Edited by Heather Howland
Cover design by Heather Howland
Cover photo by Sara Eirew

Manufactured in the United States of America

First Edition December 2015

ENTANGLED
BRAZEN

*For Margarita*

# Chapter One

A series of knots tangled in Sarge Purcell's stomach as his best friend and band manager, James, slowed his sixty-nine Mustang to a stop outside the familiar redbrick house. *Damn*, it looked smaller than the childhood home in his memory. Had his family really managed to fit inside those walls comfortably? Still, it was bigger than the impersonal motel and hotel rooms he'd been crashing in for the better part of four years. There might even be a home-cooked meal with his name on it, if he played his cards right.

Sarge put a hand out for James to shake. "I guess this is the end of the road, pal of mine. Try not to get emotional."

The always-stoic James didn't even glance in his direction. "I'm crying on the inside."

"Right." Sarge shook his head, well used to James's dry sense of humor after touring twenty-nine countries with their band Old News. Neither he nor James had anticipated staying together quite so long, both of them the epitome of a loner, but they'd ridden the wave created by Sarge's first single when he'd been fresh out of high school. James had discovered Sarge at an open-mic night, put him together with a drummer and bass player, then prayed for magic.

Crazy enough, it had worked.

An independent record label contract and five studio albums later, however, Old News was ready for a break. Not a break*up*, just a much-needed breather. With an important upcoming decision to make concerning the band's future, they were each taking some time to think. No better time than Christmas.

Which is what landed him on his sister's doorstep unannounced with a patched-up duffel bag, his guitar, an amp, and four years' worth of blown-off holidays, rushed phone calls, and all-out shitty brothering to explain.

James hit him with a long-suffering sigh from the driver's seat. "You didn't tell her you were coming, did you?"

"No, but it was strategic." Sarge adjusted the rearview mirror to point in his direction. "She's less likely to tell me to fuck off when she can see this face."

"Your face has been on the cover of a hundred magazines. Everyone is sick of it, including me."

"Yeah." A weight pressed down on Sarge's chest. "I'm kind of sick of it, too."

The two men exchanged a rare, serious glance, but looked away just as fast.

"Get out of my car." James revved the car's engine. "I'm staying in Manhattan at the Standard hotel if you need anything. Try not to, please."

Although Sarge was grateful to his manager for not pushing him to elaborate on his cryptic statement, he couldn't resist giving him a hard time. "Funny, I don't remember you saying the same thing to Lita," Sarge said, referring to Old News's female drummer and renowned troublemaker. "In fact, isn't she staying at the Standard, too? What an odd coincidence."

"Out."

Laughing to himself, Sarge pushed open the door and climbed out before removing his gear from the trunk. When it was lined up on the curb, he leaned down into the passenger-side window and rapped his knuckles on the door. "Maybe if you stopped bailing Lita out, she'd stop wreaking havoc wherever she goes."

A muscle ticked in James's jaw. "If you make a decision about the contract over the holiday, you know where to reach me. Don't wait too long. Record labels aren't known for their patience."

"Yeah. Neither are you," Sarge said, straightening. "Believe me, the contract...and everything that comes with it will be on my mind, all right? In the meantime, don't miss me too much, J."

As soon as the Mustang turned the block's corner, Sarge faced the house and let his grinning smoke screen drop. One good thing about being back in Hook, New Jersey? No one found it unusual if you looked miserable. Hell, the town's unofficial motto was, "No one escapes the Hook...might as well give up now." That sentiment had never felt truer than it did as he stared at the two-story colonial. At eighteen, he'd blown out of the godforsaken factory town not caring if he ever returned.

A broken heart and wounded pride could make a man do crazy things.

Even now, the woman responsible could be inside with his sister, drinking wine after a long day of work at their assembly-line jobs. She might be discussing her latest love interest, the way she'd done countless times while he listened from the next room. So. Many. *Times.* The hearing—the *knowing*—hadn't even been the worst part, though. Oh no. That had come when he finally entered the room and she *ruffled his hair.* Completely unaware of the jealousy storming inside him like a hurricane bent on destruction. Without a clue that he thought about her every minute of the day, even when she wasn't babysitting him.

Jasmine Taveras. His lifelong obsession and curse.

Did he want her to be inside? Hell yeah. Because four years away *should* have gotten Jasmine out of his system. That's what he'd intended when he'd bought a one-way ticket to Los Angeles after graduating from Hook High. Forgetting her. Now, however, when faced with the prospect of meeting her face-to-face, the traitorous organ within his rib cage had already found a rapid baseline, which increased in pace the more he allowed her image to surface. Jesus H. Christ. As a teenager, whenever she was breathing in his vicinity, every fiber of his biology would stretch, begging to wrap around her and harden into cement so she could never escape. He'd been too young to cope with those rushes of hormones then, but that damn sure shouldn't be the case now.

But it was. She was the reason he'd picked up a guitar freshman year of high school, wanting to be the background to that voice. Wanting to support it, enhance it, be a part of it any way he could.

Not that he'd ever told anyone. When asked by journalists, talk show hosts, or online music blogs, his answer was always the same patented mistruth. *It seemed like an easy way to get girls.* If he closed his eyes, he could see the way her lips had curled on each end the first time he'd played a string of notes on his busted Gibson. He'd played every day since, never failing to see her mouth during that first strum.

*Enough.* With a curse, Sarge snatched up his guitar case in one hand, the amp in the other, and climbed the creaking wooden stairs leading to his childhood home. His parents had transferred the deed to his sister, before retiring and moving to Florida, knowing she could use the space for raising her now-three-year-old daughter. The niece Sarge had never met in person, thanks to a demanding tour schedule.

*Damn.* Starting now, he had a shit-ton of making up to do, didn't he? With a bracing breath, Sarge lifted his fist to knock on the door, but it swung open before he got the chance. The guitar case slipped from Sarge's fingers, landing with a thud on the hollow porch. "River?"

Across the threshold, someone who resembled his sister gazed back at him, looking baffled. Baffled and *exhausted*, to be more accurate. And no—it *was* his sister. But she'd stopped dyeing her hair blond, bringing it back to woodsy brown, along with lopping off the long, bouncy ponytail that had always been her trademark. He could count on one hand the times he'd seen River without makeup since she'd hit middle school, but she didn't have an ounce of it on now. Even worse, her eyes were puffy, as if she'd been crying.

Guilt smacked Sarge in the face like a metal mallet. This wasn't a bad day she was dealing with. This was more. And he'd been completely absent. Four years' worth of absent. "Riv," he prompted. "Hey. You all right?"

A sharp, pained laugh stumbled past her lips. "Yeah. Yeah, I just—you've changed so much. I've seen you in magazines and on talk shows, but I thought it was just the cameras making you seem larger than life. I-I didn't realize you could *grow* so much after eighteen—" When she noticed the luggage at his feet, she cut herself off. "Wait. What are you doing here?"

*Pretty much feeling like a tool.* Showing up without any forewarning had felt fine ten minutes ago. It was a house with five bedrooms; surely there was a spare corner to crash. Family is family and all that. Now? His unexpected arrival on his obviously harried sister's doorstep seemed on par with puppy trafficking. "I…huh." He scratched his stubbled chin. "The band is taking some time off. I wanted to see you and meet my niece. A plan that sounded way better in my head.

Are you okay? You don't seem okay."

River's eyes widened a little…and filled with tears. Without warning, she launched herself at Sarge, throwing her arms around his neck. He barely had a chance to fold her too-skinny form in a hug before she pushed away and stepped backward into the house. "Um." She turned in a circle, as if looking for a tissue, before giving up and falling sideways against the doorjamb. "It's good to see you. The band…I still have the *SNL* performance saved in my recordings. You were amazing…I knew you would be."

The fact that she hadn't answered his question of *are you okay?* alarmed him even more. "Yeah. Thanks—"

"And I know, I *know* you've been sending the money every month and I'm *so* grateful. You have no idea—"

"Come on, Riv. Don't even mention it—"

"—but Marcy has been asking about her father." She lifted stiff fingers to her temple and rubbed with a jerky motion. "She's been asking why all the kids at school have a man at their house and she doesn't. And I can't let you stay. I can't confuse her or see her feelings get hurt when you leave, okay? I'm sorry. I'm really sorry."

A sharp object wedged just beneath his Adam's apple, then dug in a little further. What the hell had happened while he was on the road? Why hadn't his parents told him River needed more than the monthly check he'd been sending? "Of course. No…I'm an asshole for not thinking about how Marcy would react." Sarge picked up his guitar case, but made no move to leave. In a flash, it became obvious that he wouldn't be leaving Hook for a while. Not until whatever was broken with his sister was fixed. "Just tell me what you need. I'll make sure you get it."

River opened her mouth and closed it again before taking a long breath. "Look. I'm going to call Jasmine. She's got an empty room at her place and I know she wouldn't mind you using it."

There were only so many shocks to the system a man could take—and *that* one nearly knocked him out of commission. Staying in the same house as Jasmine. Seeing her, smelling her, hearing her? Everything he'd shoved down into a duct-taped box in his gut would fight its way free. He'd never be able to wrestle it back in. "No. No, don't bother. I'll find the closest motel."

River scoffed. "Yeah, I'm *so* not letting that happen. You think I'd let you stay in a motel this close to friends and family? No way."

"Listen. I'll figure something out," Sarge said with finality, glimpsing a pair of tiny neon-pink tennis shoes behind his sister, where they'd been tossed haphazardly on the stairs. "Can I...meet Marcy, at least?"

"Yes. Of *course*." Misery lurking in her expression, River reached out and squeezed his arm. "Come back Thursday night? Around dinnertime?"

"You know it."

Sensing River wouldn't like shutting the door in his face, Sarge threw her a reassuring wink and turned to head down the stairs. Laid out in front of him, the residential block where he'd spent his youth seemed unfamiliar—like a crude depiction of hazy memories penciled out by a sketch artist. The sidewalks were broken up by tree roots, the telephone lines sagging under the weight of tied-together sneakers. There was a basketball hoop in every driveway, but no kids made use of them. It was quiet, except for traffic passing on the avenue, the occasional honk or greeting being yelled through a car window.

It wasn't the first time in his life he didn't know where he was headed. But it was the first time he knew he couldn't go back. To anything. To any*where*.

"What's your next move, Purcell?" he muttered under his

breath.

Two blocks down, he could just make out the neon beer sign in the window of Hook's local dive bar, the Third Shift.

His feet were moving before a conscious decision had been made.

Yep. Times like these, a man went out and got shit-faced.

# Chapter Two

When it came to men, it was slim-ass pickings in Hook, New Jersey.

Lack of selection had to be responsible for Jasmine wearing her best dress within the Third Shift's decaying, smoke-stained walls. *Seriously.* The ramshackle joint was seconds from falling down around their ears—why didn't anyone looked concerned? Probably because each and every patron was half past wasted, shouting to be heard over a played-out Bruce Springsteen CD that always skipped on "Born to Run." Her date—if one could give him such a legitimate title—was the loudest of the local dimwits, sloshing beer over his meaty paw as he expounded on his theories concerning factory politics. She'd heard it all before. Many times. God knew she loved a working-class hero. After all, she happened to be one herself.

But...*carajo*! Sometimes she just wished they would stop complaining about life's unfairness and shut the fuck up.

If forgetting about her sweaty daily grind on the assembly line wasn't the point of going on a date with one of these dudes, what was? She'd put on a dress and lipstick to remind herself she was a woman, not just a cog in a machine. Or the outspoken coworker who was always nominated to speak on everyone's behalf to the boss man. There had been a time when she'd wanted more. Much more. Life didn't always work out the way you expected, though, and she'd learned to be content. Mostly. When she didn't think too hard about what might have been. Lofty ambitions were no longer part of her psyche, but a decent date once in a while wasn't a lot to ask.

The night had started off pretty standard. Her date, Carmine, had driven them in his pickup to an Italian restaurant in Montclair—white tablecloths, the whole nine yards. And okay, fine, he'd yapped for forty-five minutes about his idea for novelty bumper stickers that say MECHANICS HAVE BIG TOOLS, but she'd entertained herself with three glasses of red wine. This was her second date with Carmine, although the first had been months ago after which she'd told him, do better next time. It *seemed* as if he'd taken her directive to heart. She'd even considered kissing his sorry ass good-night. Then he'd gone and done it. He'd pulled up outside the Third Shift, "just for a nightcap."

What was it about the men in this town and the Third Shift? They didn't consider their day complete until they'd added their unique man scent to the mélange of questionable odors. Now he was doing this *thing*. This "reach over and massage her neck while yukking it up with his boys" thing. The kind of move you pull on a long-suffering girlfriend, and she was far from that to Carmine.

When Jasmine's cell phone buzzed inside her clutch purse and she saw River's name come up, concern replaced her irritation. It was just past bedtime for Marcy. If River was calling her, something was up.

Jasmine pressed the phone to her ear and edged away from the group of men. "Hey, Riv. Everything okay?"

"Yeah. Kind of? I don't know." A long pause. "My brother just showed up on my doorstep. Out of nowhere."

"You're *kidding*. Sarge?"

"The one and only."

A smile sprang unbidden to Jasmine's lips. She'd always had a soft spot for the kid. Forever pressed up in the corner of the Purcell family's living room, hair across one eye, playing that beat-up guitar. So quiet and thoughtful all the damn time. His steady intensity would have unnerved her on a guy so young—seven years her junior, if she recalled correctly—if he hadn't displayed on countless occasions what a massive heart was hiding underneath all those Judas Priest T-shirts. One afternoon, during the hottest summer she could remember, Jasmine had caught him leaving a plastic bag on his elderly neighbor's porch. Having assumed he was doorbell-ditching like most boys his age, she'd started to read him the riot act, until she'd seen what was inside. About a dozen old VHS tapes.

"Mrs. Grant doesn't have a DVD player, so I picked these up from the thrift store. *Gunsmoke, The Andy Griffith Show...*" he'd explained, before vanishing into his own house without giving her a chance to commend him. Yeah, she'd known Sarge would be successful at whatever career he decided on, but she'd never expected such a rapid rise to fame. For music, nonetheless. A dream she'd always harbored for herself that never came to fruition.

Her smile slipped away. When her younger self had encouraged Sarge to follow his dreams, she'd been so confident in her own abilities, positive she would ultimately be the one whose talent earned her a pass out of Hook. But it had been Sarge's destiny the whole time. God, he would pity her now. The girl who'd once been almost smug in her mentoring was now nothing more than an assembly-line fixture.

Jasmine realized she'd been silent for too long and shook

herself. "That's great, right? You'll have Sarge home for Christmas." When River released a slow breath down the line, a realization began to creep in on Jasmine's end. "Or maybe we're not happy about this." She hesitated. "Marcy?"

"Yeah. She's been asking about her father again."

Jasmine toed the ancient barroom floor, hating River's dejected tone of voice. She'd heard way too much of it lately. "What can I do?"

"I know it's a lot to ask, but can Sarge use your spare room? I can't bear the thought of him staying with strangers." River made an agonized sound. "Maybe I should have just let him stay here—"

"Of *course* he can use the room," Jasmine broke in. "Don't think any more about it. We're only a few blocks apart—it'll be just like he's home, except you won't have to pick up his socks."

A meaty arm snaked across Jasmine's shoulders, beer breath drifting along her neck. He murmured something about her dress fitting her perfectly, a sentiment that unfortunately made its way to River's ears. "Oh, Jesus. Carmine took you back to the Third Shift, didn't he?"

"A night wouldn't be complete," Jasmine answered, squirming away from her date, who instead of taking the hint, only tightened his hold. "Listen, I have to handle this. Send Sarge over with a fresh change of clothes and I'll make sure he's comfortable."

"Oh, *thank* you. You're a saint." A brief pause. "Hey, Jas? I know this goes without saying, but you can do a thousand times better than Carmine."

"Now you tell me." Jasmine's laugh was hollow as she disconnected the call and replaced the phone in her purse. *Could* she do better? She wasn't so sure. Knowing her face was in full grimace mode, she patted Carmine on the chest in a placating manner, the universal signal for *go home, you're drunk.* "'Kay, big guy. Thanks for the eats. I'm going to ask the bartender to call me a cab."

"What? No way. I've only had two friggin' beers." Ignoring her reticence, he tried to turn her into the cradle of his body. "Maybe I'm drunk on the way you look in that short dress."

"Yeah. I heard you the first time. Not for nothing, but compliments usually come at the *beginning* of a date."

"Awww, I was working up to it." He leaned in for a kiss, but she dodged him. "What's this about someone staying at your place? Won't they interrupt what we've got planned?"

"*Perdón?*" Jasmine's spine snapped into a straight line. "Of which plans do you speak? I'd answer carefully."

Her shock was obviously the opportunity Carmine needed to go in for the kill. His chapped lips stamped down onto hers, big, grabby hands tugging her closer. Without being given time to suck in a breath, she had exactly zero oxygen in her lungs to sustain her as he mashed their mouths together. Feeling the beginnings of panic when no one came to her aid, Jasmine's hand flew up and connected—*smack*—with his cheek. Once, twice. A third time.

Even after she slapped him, it took a few seconds for him to pull away. "What the *fuck,* Jasmine?" After a glance over his shoulder that found his group of buddies busting their guts laughing, Carmine's hand closed around her right biceps. Tight. *Tighter.* "You've been asking for that all night, so I finally give it to you—"

Poor Carmine never saw it coming. To be fair, neither did Jasmine. One second, she was gearing up to knee Carmine in the family jewels and the next? He was on the dingy floor with an even bigger man straddling his neck, taking a punch to the face that gave even a pissed-off Jasmine sympathy pains. She couldn't see her rescuer's face, but through her haze of shock, she had one simple yet dominant thought.

*Hello Shoulders.*

They were broad and flexing and *badass*. Shoulders that made her think of Tarzan swinging through the jungle with a tiny blond woman clinging to his toga-covered body. Soap commercial shoulders that usually had frothy suds coasting down them in delicious rivulets while the man with a big white-toothed smile on his face lathered. God. Her rescuer could barely keep them inside his white long-sleeved T-shirt.

In Jasmine's periphery, she could see a crowd was beginning to form around the brawl—a far bigger crowd than a fight usually warranted in the Third Shift. Some of them even had cell phones out, filming the action. *What gives?*

In an almost unconscious movement, Jasmine sidled around the fighting twosome to get a better look at her savior, but Carmine—finally realizing his ass was being kicked—rolled the newcomer over to lay a right cross of his own. Jasmine cringed at the thud of flesh on bone. Her date's victory was short-lived, however, because Shoulders had the edge again within a split second, pinning Carmine down with a forearm to the throat, leaning down to get in his face.

"Took her three slaps to make you stop? Are you *serious*?" He pressed harder on Carmine's jugular. "When a woman hits you, that's a pretty accurate signal that she's not into it." A left hook crunched the cartilage in her date's nose. "You know who else isn't into it? *Me*. Can you tell?"

Carmine's eyes were wide as saucers as he struggled to breath. Or speak. It was hard to tell since Shoulders commanded Jasmine's attention. There was a familiarity about the newcomer…but she couldn't know him. A woman remembered raw, commanding men like him. Men who spoke with conviction. They were a rare breed, and if she'd made his acquaintance, it would have stuck.

Out of the corner of her eye, Jasmine saw Carmine's buddies set down their brews and hasten toward the fight, obviously intending to intervene. Jasmine stepped into their path, holding up a staying hand while tapping Shoulders with the other one. "Look, I really appreciate this, but you better take off before it's five on one."

Jasmine swore his wide, muscled back shivered beneath her touch. "What?" His tone was amused. "You wouldn't be in my corner?"

God, that voice. Comforting *and* thrilling. Smooth *and* gritty. "You're right, it would be five on two. I'll take the bald one. He has a bum knee."

His head turned just slightly, enough that she could see the rugged stubble on his chin, the strength of his profile. "I appreciate the offer, but you're done fighting off men for the night." As if pissed at the reminder of Carmine's treatment, he cursed under his breath, regarding his opponent like a slime-covered slug. "When I let you speak, your first words better be an apology. We clear?"

Carmine's eyes shot irate sparks, but after a beat, he nodded. Her rescuer removed his hold and stood, yanking Carmine to his feet by the shirt collar. "Sorry," Carmine spat in her direction just as his friends reached them. Jasmine automatically tried to insert herself between Shoulders and the drunk locals, but he seemed to anticipate her move, grabbing her wrist and holding her away.

The men squared off for a tense moment before Carmine's bald friend tilted his head one way, then the other. "Hold up. Sarge Purcell?" He elbowed Carmine in the ribs, who grunted and doubled over. "Old News. It's the guy from Old News. I fuckin' *love* that band, man."

While everyone in the bar seemed to swell closer, repositioning themselves to get a better look at Shoulders with cell phone cameras at the ready, Jasmine's jaw hit the floor in utter astonishment. Nuh-uh. No way in Hook was this giant enforcer with Tarzan body parts the kid she used to babysit. When he'd left Jersey, he'd been eighteen. Tall, sure.

Handsome, yeah, okay. But growth spurts the likes of this weren't possible, were they? She'd seen him on TV, of course. But television-size and life-size were two very different things, apparently, because Sarge had been remodeled from a one-story colonial into a big brick mansion.

Jasmine slid her grip around his elbow, noticing his muscles go taut, but too curious to analyze that reaction. She turned him around to face her and couldn't stop the words poised on her tongue from stage diving. "Hol-y, hol-y shit."

Sarge Purcell had turned into a man while he'd been gone.

And when he stepped closer, forcing her head back, and ran intelligent blue eyes over her face, Jasmine realized she needed to block all further thoughts pertaining to shoulders or Tarzan or soap rivulets. Those thoughts made her a pervert, didn't they? *Claro que sí.* Of course they did. Worse than a woman who simply found a too-young man attractive in passing, because she'd *known* Sarge as a preteen for God's sake. Ribbed him when he shaved for the first time and nicked his face in ten different places.

Oh, but there was nothing left of that preteen inside this man with the bleeding lip and a five o'clock shadow. Until he stopped drilling her with those baby blues and smiled, the edge of his mouth kicking up just a notch. There he was. Thank God. *Deep breaths, girl.*

"You still know how to pick 'em, huh, Jasmine?"

"Hmm—what?"

Sarge jerked his chin toward Carmine. "You shouldn't be in this place, with that guy, looking so pretty."

*You babysat him. You babysat him.* "Turned into quite a smooth operator on the road, didn't you?"

A little bit of light left his eyes. "Something like that."

Why did she feel guilty all of a sudden? Shaking herself out of the weird trancelike state she was encapsulated in, Jasmine forced a welcoming smile onto her face. The kind you gave to the sweet kid you were babysitting when you'd brought him cookies as a surprise. "Word on the street is you're staying with me tonight."

His headshake was unrushed. "No. I'm not."

A little insulted, Jasmine poked him in the chest, declining to consciously acknowledge he was hard as granite. "What? You're too much of a star now to stay in my tiny two-bedroom apartment?"

A rain cloud moved across his face. "It's not like that."

"What's it like?" Jasmine didn't take any pleasure from delivering the guilt trip, but she needed to come through for River. Her single-mother friend had been dealing with far too much lately without wondering if her brother was spending the holiday in an impersonal hotel room. Even though the thought of Sarge's mile-wide frame squeezing through her front door gave her an uncomfortable case of nerves.

She needed to stick to a game plan. As of now, that game plan was to treat this hot rock-star ass like the twelve-year-old boy in her memory. And if she was worried he would look around at her meager possessions and throw sympathy in her direction, she had to put it aside for tonight. "You still like grilled cheese? Come over and I'll make you one."

He barked a laugh. "Jasmine, I just handed your date his ass. How's about you start treating me like I'm twenty-two?"

Twenty-two. *Jesus.* She'd still had stars in her eyes at that age. Ready to take on all comers. Giving the finger to anyone who said *you can't do it.* But Sarge? Sarge *had* done it. "You might be older now, but you're still a kid compared to me. I'll be thirty years old—"

"The day after Christmas." He'd obviously surprised himself with the interjection, but hid it with a cough into his fist. "I know."

He wasn't the only one nursing shock that he'd remembered her birthday. Damn, *she* was usually the one putting people through their paces, but Sarge two-point-ohhhh couldn't seem to stop surprising her. "Look, it's late. If you want to find another, fancier place to lay your head tomorrow, I won't stop you. But your sister asked me for a favor and that means I'll drag you home caveman-style tonight, if necessary. So what's it going to be?"

"There you are, Jas," Sarge murmured before pausing to consider her. "All right. Let's go."

# Chapter Three

Funny enough, among the three band members that made up Old News, Sarge was considered the levelheaded decision-maker. The planner. The one who reminded everyone to get at least an hour of sleep the night before a show. That wasn't to say he didn't occasionally drink his body weight and tell his deepest secrets to a convenient ficus, but considering the spoils at his disposal, he was almost embarrassingly well behaved for someone *NME Magazine* had deemed "Rock's Naughty Prince."

That title, however, hadn't come courtesy of his behavior. Oh no. It was the song lyrics he wrote. He'd dug himself a deep hole on the first album, nearly every song about wanting to—well…have sex. Have sex with *Jasmine* to be specific. Since he'd never been the type to discuss his feelings out loud—potted plants notwithstanding—he'd written them down. He'd written *everything* down. Needs, fantasies, observations about how Jasmine filled out a bathing suit that he'd had no right to make.

Four years had given him a little clarity on what his mind-set had been at eighteen, the year he'd grown sick of watching her date men who didn't deserve her. Thinking she'd finally acknowledge him as a man, but realizing that eventuality was nothing more than a pipe dream. God, he'd hoped like hell never to go back there. To that deeply fucked-up, needy place where his dick filled the leg of his boxers just from looking at her. To the place where his heart rammed itself against his tonsils, mind racing, trying to figure out what she'd say next. How he could respond to make her smile.

In town less than a goddamn hour and he was already there. The difference being, now he knew how to satisfy a woman, knew how to make her achieve pleasure with the use of his body. And having that knowledge somehow made it worse to look, but not touch.

Sitting beside him in the cab was the woman he'd been in cataclysmic lust with since middle school. She was bright-eyed from too much wine, her tight red dress was snug around her crossed thighs…and she was giving him a patient babysitter smile from across the cracked leather seat.

Being the calm, objective individual his bandmates knew him to be, he shouldn't be perceiving Jasmine's amused expression as a dare. A goad. Ah, but he did. Four years hadn't changed a single thing—but maybe it didn't have to stay that way. Maybe he could fight his way free of this permanent straitjacket she'd laced him into eons ago by accepting that dare in her eyes. Throwing down his own gauntlet. Finally indulging his fantasy and then kissing it good-bye, once and for all.

*Bad idea.* Such a *bad* fucking idea. She'd flung a spear straight through his chest once, and four years hadn't made her any less capable of doing it again. Two new songs had already written themselves since they'd met eyes at the Third Shift, another one halfway composed in his head. Could he remain mentally detached enough to work his way free of her spell if things were to get physical? Wasn't living free of Jasmine haunting him worth the risk?

There was only one way to know for sure.

"That bloody lip looks pretty ugly," Jasmine said. "Does it hurt much?"

Sarge ran his tongue along the inside of his bottom lip, encountering the metallic tang of blood. He hadn't even been aware of the injury, probably too distracted by a certain someone in sky-high heels. God, he was a mess. "I would say, 'You should see the other guy,' but I don't think you should. See him again, that is."

On the other side of the plastic partition, the cab driver whistled low under his breath and received an arched eyebrow from Jasmine. "I'd already decided that before you cleaned his clock, but your concern is duly noted."

"Good."

She breathed into her hands, rubbing them together for warmth. "You've changed a lot. I remember when I couldn't drag a single word out of you."

Remembering the way he used to clam up, losing all ability to speak at the sight of her in his living room, he wished he could go back in time and tell that kid to grow some courage. He had it now. In spades. It was time she knew about it. "Maybe I was just saving the words up."

"For your songs." A gorgeous smile lit up her face, one that was unique to Jasmine. She never showed her teeth, just pursed her lips in a way that plumped them, her eyes tilting at the ends. It made you her instant coconspirator. Or if you were Sarge, it sent a giant moose stampeding through your stomach. "When they come over the loudspeaker on the factory floor, everyone sings. Before you, they only ever did that for Bruce. And pre-country Bon Jovi."

Sarge felt his lips tug at the image. "What about you? Do you sing when they come on?"

Her smile wavered. "No. But not because I don't like your songs," she rushed to add, mischief lurking in her eyes. "I just don't want to show anyone up."

Something about the way she said it made Sarge question her truthfulness. Which made no damn sense, since he knew Jasmine's voice was incredible. If he closed his eyes and thought back to hazy Hook summers spent at the community pool or drinking Coke in his backyard, he could hear her voice, husky and confident, floating in a jumble with the humidity.

They pulled up in front of Jasmine's building, the cab's brakes protesting as it slowed to a stop along the curb. Sarge paid with a twenty before Jasmine could extricate her purse, earning him a narrow-eyed frown. "Sarge—"

"What?" His tone was teasing. "How else am I going to repay you for this forced hospitality?"

Jasmine didn't answer as they climbed out of opposite ends of the cab, meeting at the glass-door entrance of her apartment building after Sarge retrieved his gear from the trunk. "I did you a favor. The closest motel rents by the hour."

"I've been in worse," he murmured, following her into the building. "How long have you been living here?"

She went to punch the elevator call button, but slumped when she saw the OUT OF SERVICE sign taped over the sliding metal doors. Indicating the stairwell with a nod, she headed in that direction and Sarge followed, not managing to keep his gaze from gliding up her calves, the backs of her smooth thighs. "My second year at the factory...when it became obvious I would be here for a while."

Sarge allowed her to ascend a few stairs before climbing after her. "You don't like the factory?"

Her laugh punctuated the air. "No one likes the factory except the suited boys upstairs. If you'd left poor Carmine alone a few minutes longer, you would have heard all about it."

"I'm good with my decision," he responded too quickly. Just hearing her say the asshole's name made him grind his teeth. He still couldn't believe she'd been struggling in a bar full of men and no one had come to her aid. To be fair, each and every patron had been intoxicated, and Jasmine had been in an alcove where he might have missed her, had the voice from his dreams not reached out and slugged him the second he walked into the Third Shift.

Sarge wasn't sure his reaction would have differed if Jasmine had been *into* the kiss with Carmine. He'd just wanted the guy off her. Period.

Sarge glanced up in time to see Jasmine watching him over her shoulder, tugging down her skirt as she bypassed the second-floor entrance and headed for the third. Did she sense his inability to avert his gaze when her hips were swaying like a checkered flag at the beginning of a race? That red hem couldn't be deterred on its mission to slip higher and higher, where it teased the underside of her ass. The fog of jealousy that had descended at the mention of her date's name was being burned away by an increasing weight between his legs. So much sharper than usual because the source of his hottest fantasies was leading him to her apartment. The place she slept, showered, touched herself.

*Ah, Jesus. Don't think about that.*

"So…" Jasmine slipped her fingers beneath the dress's hem once again, holding it in place at a modest level. "How long are you in town?"

Sarge followed her through the beige metal door onto the building's third level, watching as she searched for her keys in the clutch purse. "Long enough to forget why we were starting to annoy each other, I'm guessing." When she laughed over her shoulder, eyes sparkling, he had to take a second to regroup. "Our drummer, Lita, was getting into too much trouble on the road, so our manager put her in a time-out. And I've waited long enough to meet Marcy. Christmas seemed like the best time."

A weight pressed down on his shoulders. "We're also on the fence about signing with a new label. It would mean more studio time, a quick turnaround on another tour…"

"That's incredible," Jasmine breathed, pausing midstep. "Why would you ever turn something like that down?"

*It doesn't matter how far I travel, my head is always here.* "No reason. We'll probably sign." Sarge threaded his fingers through his hair. "So what's my niece like?"

"Ohh. You're going to love her. She's a miniature River." Jasmine pushed into the apartment and flipped on a lamp with a pink shade, casting the living room in a rosy glow. "So. Lita, huh?" She turned with crossed arms, waggling her eyebrows at him. "Is she your girlfriend?"

Sarge tried to contain his horror and couldn't. "She's like my kid sister." He set his bag down and circled the apartment, trying not to be obvious about inhaling the sight of everything she touched on a daily basis. "A kid sister who can drink me under the table. And then bury me under her rap sheet."

He couldn't see Jasmine's reaction because she turned and disappeared into the kitchen. For a full ten count, Sarge could only watch the doorway, his old self warning him that being in tight spaces with Jasmine was a bad idea. But he wasn't the old Sarge anymore. This trip could be his only opportunity to kick this infatuation. *Don't waste it.*

Sarge followed Jasmine, coming to an abrupt stop on the threshold when he saw Jasmine heating up a pan. And removing the fixings to make a grilled cheese.

Something unruly danced inside his rib cage, begging to get out and run free. He couldn't even appreciate the truly gorgeous fucking image of Jasmine at the stove, her waist flaring into hips in need of gripping, her long black hair falling in waves down her back. All he could process was irritation.

It might have been unintentional, but with one gesture, she'd sent him back to the misery of his teen years. Being babied by a woman who inspired sweaty, wicked images at inopportune moments of his day. Sending him to the school bathroom to work out the ever-present lust wrought by his older infatuation. It had never gone away, no matter how many times he'd tried to appease himself. Every day had left him feeling raw and exposed—kind of like he felt right now.

He refused to sink any deeper.

He advanced into the kitchen and scooped the cheese singles off the counter, intending to put them back in the fridge. "No need to go to the trouble, Jas. I'm not hungry."

"Ah, come on." She peeked up at him from beneath thick eyelashes, a sly smile decorating her lips. The easy comfort she projected was completely at odds with the precise bread-buttering taking place in her hands. Was she nervous around him? The possibility sank like an anchor in his stomach, but he wasn't given the chance to fix it, because it happened. "You're always hungry," she said quietly, before setting down the bread knife, turning to face him...and ruffling his hair.

Sarge's mind attempted to overrule his body, which swelled to life like the tide during a full moon. What he wanted to do painted itself in vivid detail behind his eyes. Snatch a hand out to circle her wrist and pin it against the small of her back. To overwhelm her. To chastise her for trying to knock his vital years of experience from their perch. He wanted to watch Jasmine's back arch out of necessity, tilt her tits up, mashing those pointed peaks against his chest, and *fuck*... that's when he would start praying that her answering sob of surprise would shake free those mounds from her dress.

He didn't act on any of that, however, because she'd already been held against her will tonight, and he would dive headfirst into an early grave before he fell into the date from hell's category. Inaction wasn't a possibility, though, either.

Fuck no. Whether or not he'd anticipated it upon returning to Hook, tonight had been a long time coming, and he wouldn't let the chance go to waste. With a quick dip forward, Sarge scooped up Jasmine and deposited her on the kitchen counter, adjacent to the stove, coming up between her splayed thighs. When her ass landed on the beige Formica, her red lips parted on a startled gasp, tits bouncing with the impact, right beneath his mouth. *Christ.*

With a steel will, Sarge reined in the moan of a man finally granted conjugal visits after a decade in prison. It was right there, imprisoned in his throat, all thanks to having Jasmine so close. Feeling her body heat. Listening to her inhale.

"What are you— W-what was that?"

He pressed his knuckled fists into the counter on either side of her hips and leaned in, close enough to see her irises dilate. "I'm making you the grilled cheese this time around. How's about that?"

An adorable wrinkle formed between her brows. "I already ate."

"I'm aware." Dragging himself away was a feat, but the image of her on a date with Carmine induced enough annoyance to make it possible. He could feel her attention following him closely as he picked up where she'd left off with the grilled cheese, slipping two slices of cheddar between the white bread and dropping it onto the well-heated pan. The two minutes it took to cook the sandwich simmered with tension, amplified by their lack of conversation. Not to mention, Jasmine's drawing attention to her toned thighs by tugging on the hem of her dress, writhing that delicious ass on the counter to keep it pulled down. They met eyes as she performed the sexy maneuver, and he swore her breath hitched, but couldn't be sure, thanks to the sizzle of the pan.

"I'm really not hungry," she muttered as he flopped the grilled cheese onto a plate and cut it in half.

Sarge lifted one half to his mouth and blew on the edge, all the while easing back toward her at the counter. When he was inches away, her knees shot back together, but he let his lower abdomen rest against them anyway, wanting—*needing*—to see how she would react. But she stayed still, a wealth of caution radiating from her tense form. Those deep brown eyes seemed to liquefy as she focused in on his mouth…and that was all she wrote. His hard-on grew more prominent in his jeans, contouring to the curve of his fly. Again, that desperate moan climbed in his throat, the one that would give him away as a man obsessed, but he staved it off. The need to jerk himself off had been this intense only one other time in his life, and it had involved Jasmine in a glittery gold bikini, oiling herself up on a towel in his backyard. He'd been seventeen—Jasmine, twenty-four—and after five minutes of watching the torture from his bedroom window, he'd laid face down in his bed and come, groaning into his pillow, after two frantic pumps.

Now, Sarge lifted the sandwich to her mouth, letting the crust brush against the seam of her plump lips. "Eat it for me." Of its own accord, his left hand dropped to her ankle, teasing the inside with back and forth brushes of his thumb. "I don't want your last meal tonight to be one that guy paid for. Not while I'm in town."

Brown eyes clashed with blue. "I don't think…eating this particular meal is a very good idea."

His thumb dipped into her shoe, sliding along the arch of her foot. "It's just a sandwich, Jas. Humor me?"

The more pressure he applied to the sensitive section of her foot, the more her eyelids fluttered, but after a moment of the treatment, she shook her head and sat up straighter. "No, it's not just a sandwich. It's you forcing me to admit I made a bad decision in terms of who I date." She pushed away the grilled cheese. "I'm fine admitting that to myself, but not someone else. You're judging."

She tried to slide off the counter, but on impulse, Sarge stepped between her legs at the last minute, forcing her to slide down his lap to the floor. It was a big fucking mistake, even though the answering bliss in his groin as her pussy slid over the bulge behind his zipper felt nothing like one. Still, it ripped the Band-Aid off the moan he'd managed to cage since entering her apartment. It released against the top of her head like feedback from a hot microphone. He could practically feel the facade he'd been attempting tumble to the floor in a heap…but that wasn't all he felt. Jasmine's petite curves shivered against him, almost violently, a call his body answered by pressing her back against the counter, his fists lifting to bash against the overhead cabinets.

He heard her gulp, followed by wavering but determined words. "Whatever this is, it's not happening. I won't let it." She shifted against him, her shuddering exhale fanning his collarbone when he only pressed closer to keep her from rubbing against his cock, which would cause all hell to break loose in his jeans. "Sarge. W-*what* is this? You're my…best friend's kid brother."

Finally, he found the power to speak around the arousal clawing along his spine. His mouth was a centimeter from hers now, but he had no memory of when he'd moved. Both sets of their lips were parted, hot, hurried breaths clashing between them. "I haven't been a kid for a damn long while, Jasmine. You want to feel it again and make sure?"

Her lips parted in shock, pink appearing on her cheeks. "*Sarge.*"

He recognized that tone as her stern, no-nonsense, I'll-tell-your-*parents*-about-this-behavior tone, and it propelled him to take his warning a little further, even though something told him she was working *hard* to pull off her disapproving attitude. "No more fixing me sandwiches. No more ruffling my goddamn hair." He reached down and grasped her hand, bringing it to the back of his head, moving it in a messy circle. "If I ever feel your fingers in my hair again, they'd better be pulling my face closer to whatever I'm licking."

The sound that tumbled from her lips was part sob, part hiccup, hands scrabbling against his shoulders to push him away. He let her go, because she needed to know *he* would always stop when she indicated he should. Always. No matter how much it ached to stop touching her.

The hand Jasmine shoved through her dark hair shook, but her voice was steel. "You can't just *talk* to me like that."

Honestly, he wanted to laugh up at the cracked ceiling. She obviously hadn't been paying close attention to his song lyrics. "Look, I say what I'm thinking now. Keeping it to myself never did me much good."

"Oh yeah?" She kicked off her high heels in the direction of the tiny dining alcove, near the kitchen's entrance. "Well, it'll do *me* some good."

Sarge crossed his arms, smiling inwardly as an idea presented itself. "Fine. You'll get no more gutter mouth from me as long as I'm in town."

Her chin lifted, but she was suspicious. "Thanks…"

"But you have to take a bite of this sandwich." He felt the amusement slip from his expression, but couldn't stop it from going. Yeah, it was important to him that her last meal not be from some unworthy son of a bitch. But there was a darker part of him that wanted to fall asleep knowing he'd put something he'd made in her stomach. Ah, come on, who was he kidding? He wouldn't sleep a damn second tonight. It would take him an hour to figure out how to wring his cock out without her hearing across the hall. And if the past were any indication, once wouldn't be enough where Jasmine was concerned. "What's it going to be?" he asked, his voice having dropped around fifty octaves.

"Oh for the love of…" Jasmine stomped across the kitchen barefoot, obviously uncaring that her tits were bouncing like sweet little temptations as she went. Sarge stepped closer as she took the bite, swallowing a growl when her teeth sank into the bread and she chewed, swallowing a few seconds later. "Happy?"

God, he wanted to smear the lipstick painting her mouth. Over to her chin, across her cheek, down her belly. "You have no idea."

She held up a single finger. "That sounded like gutter mouth in disguise."

"You know me so well."

Jasmine paused at the kitchen's threshold, one hand lingering on the frame as she perused him over her shoulder. "I thought I did."

# Chapter Four

Jasmine never had trouble sleeping. Since childhood, she'd had the ability to black out as soon as her head hit the pillow. Couch armrests, car doors, and folded arms were all fair game. At the factory, she was famous for catnaps in the break room while vending machines vended and employees chattered. So there was just no excuse for being wide-awake with three glasses of wine in her system. Dreamland should have been an easy destination, reached in mere seconds, but no. No, she had a too-young man with an ambitious mouth right across the dark, narrow hallway.

There wasn't a chance—*negative* chances, in fact—that Sarge could back up the talk with the walk. She'd dated plenty of men who spoke a big game and failed to handle business in downtown Ladyville.

Oh, but he'd been so convincing. So specific. There had been knowledge in those baby blues she didn't recall from before. Honestly, she didn't recall that kind of *try-me-you'll-love-me* attitude from anyone she'd spent time with. Coupled with that moan? That moan that made her body feel like an object to be lusted after? In the mirror across the room, she could see herself in her white nightshirt, and the image sent a flush climbing her neck. Nipples distended against the cotton material, lips parted as she struggled to regain composure. So very non-Jasmine.

*Coño. Knock it off.* It was River's brother she was thinking about. She'd attended his middle and high school graduations when she was already in her twenties. This little bud of attraction—and it *was* little…teeny tiny, minuscule, a speck, really—she'd felt between her thighs when the silk of her underwear had slipped down his rigid fly, it had to have been a fluke. An unwelcome one.

Jasmine went on occasional dates, enjoyed male companionship, and afterward, she slept the sleep of angels. No second-guessing her actions or wondering what would happen when the sun came up. No replaying interactions or trying to recapture the feel of a man's body with a now-scandalized pillow. God, if anyone in Hook knew she was lusting after a man seven years her junior—a famous musician nonetheless—she would never live it down. Everyone in this town had a long memory, and they remembered just-watch-me-blow-this-town-and-your-mind Jasmine. What's more, they remembered her failure to succeed almost as well as she did. They would view her taking up with Sarge as an attempt to recapture her youth—the future she'd never lived up to—and she wouldn't be able to stand the sympathy that would garner.

Especially if it turned out they were right. Less than a week until her thirtieth birthday, she could be having a one-third-of-life crisis. There was simply no other way to explain why she felt like she might suffocate if a certain honor-defending, potty-mouthed musician didn't follow through on his threats.

She sighed. Tomorrow, he would find another place to

crash and she could put the embarrassing crisis behind her, never telling another soul as long as she lived. *Poof.* It would be gone. Never happen—

"You awake in there, too, Jas?"

Jasmine's back arched on the bed as Sarge's voice shimmered along her spine, down the small of her back. God, had she been breathing heavily? Had she voiced her inexcusable thoughts out loud?

"I know you are," he continued, his tone dark and teasing.

"How?" Jasmine answered, before her brain could intercede.

Sarge was silent a moment, but when he spoke, he sounded different. More... *aware.* Heated. "I can hear your legs moving in the sheets."

Jasmine turned her face into the pillow to release an unsteady breath. "You shouldn't be listening that closely."

Another heavy beat passed. "Who's to decide what we shouldn't do?"

*Lord save me from this guy.* Had this seductively masculine man been hiding under the surface the entire time she'd known him, just waiting for an almighty growth spurt to make the results known? Because goddamn, someone needed to alert Guinness to make Sarge's changes a matter of public record. Her eighteen-year-old self would have called him "diesel" and sucked her teeth when he walked by. "Do you always have trouble sleeping?" Jasmine asked weakly.

"No," came his voice. "The trouble usually comes when I'm awake."

Crazy enough, she knew exactly what he meant. Sleep was the time to block everything out. Forget all the self-doubt and fear of the future and just...drop off for a while. But why would Sarge have a need to block out anything? He was internationally renowned, loved, and emulated for his work. If she'd reached his heights, she would never want to sleep again. "Maybe it'll help if you play your guitar." No answer for long minutes. "Sarge?"

"I can play you something, but I can't sing."

She arched an eyebrow toward the ceiling. "Why not?"

His laugh sent her right hand fluttering to her belly, where it flattened and rubbed in a needy circle. "You banned me from using my gutter mouth around you."

Her hand stilled. "All your songs require gutter mouth?"

"All of them," Sarge said huskily, making the darkness pulse around her.

Before she could stop herself, Jasmine trailed her fingertips up her stomach, to the valley between her breasts. No one could see her. It was fine. The shame was hers alone to bear. "Fine. Just play something slow."

For the next few minutes, she could hear Sarge getting out of bed and padding over to his luggage before flipping open the locks on his guitar case. The guest bed creaked as he sat back down and plucked a few strings. A trail of cohesive notes danced in the air, accompanied by his steady breathing, the gentle tap of his hand against the wooden instrument, as he kept time. The melody was so bold and full—almost tangible—she could feel every pluck of the strings in her middle, deep, deep, *deep* down. She tried to keep her legs still in the sheets, but they wouldn't stop moving with the beats and pauses. Her eyes drifted shut, heightening her sense of hearing…and swore his intakes of air grew shorter as the music swelled.

*Ay Dios.* The music wasn't the only thing swelling. The seams of her underwear felt abrasive against her sensitive areas, so close to the epicenter of need at the juncture of her thighs. When it occurred to Jasmine that a whispered plea into the darkness could bring Sarge into her bedroom, where he would weigh her down with his aggressively hot body, she almost gave in and used restless fingers to stroke at the thrumming ache. But the music cut out suddenly, the abrupt silence having the effect of a fluorescent light being flipped on.

"Why did you stop?" Jasmine called, when she'd regained her relative composure. "I liked that one."

She thought she heard Sarge say something in the neighborhood of *you should,* but couldn't be positive. Her eyelids were beginning to droop, even as the sounds of Sarge replacing his guitar in its case filled the small apartment. How odd that the song had relaxed her, even as it excited her body. But the oddity of the situation lay in the fact that it didn't feel odd at all. A mixture of comfort and confusion seemed to fit perfectly with her new perception of Sarge.

Jasmine reached for the forever-unused pillow propped beside her on the bed, wedging it between her thighs in an attempt to cull the rush of sensation. Just before she drifted off, she heard Sarge say, "That was the last censored version you're getting, Jas."

Her pulse skittered in her veins, sending her into tumultuous, heated, and forbidden dreams. They were full of disjointed groans and grabbing hands. Gratified grunts and straining bodies. A man was there, grappling for the upper hand, but her dream self continued to close her eyes— attempting to block him out—while luring him closer with her body. Until...oh God, until he grew tired of her mixed signals and struggled her into submission. Pinning her wrists at her sides, his hair dragging a trail over her belly button as he licked down to a core that had never felt so empty.

"Fill me," Jasmine breathed, waking herself as the words echoed like a shout in a tunnel. Sweat was still warm on her skin, shock working its way into her conscious to find the room illuminated by daylight. A quick check of her clock told her she'd woken before her alarm, something she never did.

*Thank God.* A fluttering hand found her damp chest. The

last thing she needed when she felt so primed for pleasure, so rattled with the ferocity of her dreams, was to come face-to-face with the newly minted man who she feared had somehow inspired them, although she'd be damned before saying it out loud.

Jasmine's toes were still curled when they met the cool hardwood floor. Her knees shook a little as she stood, slipped from the room, and beelined for the bathroom, refusing to spare so much as a glance into the guest room. A quick shower had her feeling somewhat refreshed, but pulling on her soft, worn-in jeans was a separate issue altogether. They slid up freshly shaven legs like a caress, folding her around her hips and backside like a squeeze from two hands. Putting on her basic cotton bra chafed her sensitive nipples, sending her teeth burrowing into an already-chewed-on bottom lip to hold in the resulting whimper.

Across the hallway, the partially open guest room was an eight-hundred-pound gorilla, taunting her, tempting her to take just a quick look at the six-foot-two man inhabiting her Ikea spare bed, but she somehow resisted. God, she really needed to get out of the apartment before Sarge woke up. For whatever reason, he seemed determined to throw her off-balance, and her game was already knocked askew this morning.

Jasmine tiptoed to the apartment's front door and made an absent grab for her keys on the console table—and came up empty. The lining of her stomach burned hot when she remembered where she'd left them. Yesterday, while getting ready for her date, she'd swapped her regular purse for the clutch she stored in the guest room closet. Her car keys—along with the multitude of spare keys to her parents' house and River's—were still inside, as they hadn't fit inside the tiny clutch. If she wanted to make it to work on time—and there was no choice if she didn't want her pay docked—she'd have to venture into the spare room to retrieve the damn keys.

"Shit." Jasmine walked in a circle. "Shit."

She took a bracing breath. This was no big deal. She'd just walk inside, grab the purse, and mosey on out. Ignoring the startlingly magnetic rock star in her bed might be difficult, but she worked an assembly line for eight grueling hours a day. This would be gravy.

"You got this, girl," she murmured, walking on the balls of her feet toward the guest room. Not wanting to chance the door creaking, she slipped in sideways through the opening, attempting to keep her eyes on the prize, also known as the purse on the bedside table. One step, two—

Sarge muttered something in his sleep and turned over on the bed. Everything south of Jasmine's breastbone tugged. Don't look…don't look…

She looked. And her chin fell.

Sarge took up the entire queen-size bed, one foot dangling off the end, the other raised higher, thanks to his bent right leg having fallen open, pointing away from Jasmine. Oh no. He was…completely and dangerously naked, nary a sheet to cover him as they'd all been kicked to the farthest reaches of the bed. Just *all* of him out there for the world to see, if the world were capable of sitting inside her tiny apartment. And sweet mother of heaven, he was a revelation. It wasn't just his overall big, rugged, sleeping-bear vibe that turned her ovaries into a funnel cloud. It wasn't his sturdy, muscular thighs, his tattoo-wrapped biceps, or his egg carton stomach, either. That would have been quite enough to keep her in fantasy material for years.

It was his…manhood. There really wasn't a more accurate term to describe it. Jasmine had seen *dicks* in her lifetime. In real life and on her laptop screen. What Sarge had going on was so very much more. It sprouted from a dark patch of hair at the top of his spread thighs and it…lounged against his abdomen like a brawny ruler, looking down on his subjects. He was aroused. Very much so. In a way that she could relate to after the fevered dreams she'd only so recently woken from. It had to be a trick of her overwrought imagination, but she swore she could see the thick vein pulsing along the underside of his distended flesh, swore it beat in time with her pulse.

Dampness spread between her legs, more noticeable and swift than she'd ever encountered before. The need to touch herself and find relief became tantamount. Choppy breathing was a disjointed echo in her ears, telling her it needed to be now. Now. Now.

But not here. No way. Not where Sarge would see her and know how she'd been affected. Although "affected" was such a silly term for the pressing need to use her fingers on the rapidly dampening flesh inside her underwear.

The car. It would have to be her car.

More than a little irritated that she'd been reduced to auto-masturbation, but too turned on to talk herself off the ledge, Jasmine took a few hurried steps, snatched up the keys and spun toward the door —

"Jas?" came Sarge's sleep-roughened voice behind her. "What…?"

Knowing she absolutely shouldn't, but apparently residing in a self-destructive realm that morning, she peeked over her shoulder, her desire taking on a whole new meaning. Sarge, clearly regaining more and more consciousness by the moment, had wrapped his hand around his erection, abs flexing as he attempted to sit up. Then he did something that seemed to suspend all time and space.

His fist descended in one single hip-thrusting stroke as he watched her.

*Mother of God.*

Jasmine booked it, chanting the words "too young, too

young, too young" as she slammed out of the apartment and down the stairwell to the parking lot, located behind the building. A tremor ran through her hand as she unlocked the car and slipped into the passenger seat, her breath puffing out white in front of her. She didn't bother putting the keys in the ignition. There was no time. She simply tossed them on the passenger seat, fumbling with breathless anticipation to unzip jeans pulled on with such resolve minutes earlier. Resolve that incinerated with the act of slipping seeking fingers down the front of her panties.

"Yes. Oh *God*," Jasmine moaned as her middle finger and forefinger met her clit. Her chest heaved, thighs widening as she treated the starved bud to quick, no-nonsense strokes. The quickening that began in her loins was immediate and powerful, a thunderbolt across a black night sky. Her flesh grew slippery beneath the pads of her fingers, the sounds of her gasps bouncing off the car's interior. The orgasm loomed as her heels pressed down, digging into the driver's side footwell. Christ, she just needed to take the edge off before it sharpened any further—

The passenger side door opened, jolting Jasmine on the seat. She knew it was Sarge. She knew the moment cool air invaded the car and purred over her fevered skin, yet did nothing to cool her need. Looking toward the passenger side to confirm he'd followed her was pointless—deep down she'd known he'd come, hadn't she?—so Jasmine threw her head back on the seat as the door clicked closed, eyes sealed shut.

Her own wrist was circled by a rough, masculine hold and yanked free of her underwear. One slow-motion beat passed. Two. Almost as if he was waiting for her to protest, but she'd shut down her better judgment in favor of almighty relief. As long as she didn't open her eyes. She would hold on to *that* safeguard at all costs, despite the fact that it only made sense to her overwrought mind.

She heard Sarge's weight shift closer on the neighboring seat…and—callused fingers dragged over her shuddering belly. Lower, lower until they met the pulsing bud begging for attention between her legs, teasing with a light downward rub that nonetheless set off a bomb blast inside her. Jasmine's broken moan pierced the air, answered by Sarge's guttural grunt, making her future climax burn even brighter, more intense as he shoved his mouth up against her ear and shook out a scalding breath.

"Liked what you saw, baby?"

*Yes. Goddammit, yes.* Jasmine stabbed her teeth into her bottom lip to contain the harsh sentiment, praying her silence wouldn't make him stop. The car's interior seemed to close in around her, the sounds of passing traffic on the nearby street doing nothing to detract from the extreme sense of airlessness. Stark, enfolding intimacy. They were the only two people awake, right here, right now, and she would die if he didn't deliver what she needed. There was no chance of that, though, because Sarge's mouth found the skin behind her ear and introduced it to his tongue, just as two big fingers slid down on either side of her clit, caging sacred flesh between rough knuckles.

"This is what I've been chasing. *Fuck*. Right here. You want to know how long you've been teasing me with this pussy?" A light pinch of her nub made her knees jerk together on a gasp. "I'm going to tell you anyway, but a *yes* would make my cock harder. Say yes—now—so I can replay it later and pretend you're whispering it from your knees and unzipping my goddamn jeans."

"You're—" Jasmine broke off as he shoved his middle finger into her heat, pushing deeper until she screamed his name. Even then, he didn't stop, grinding his fist against her damp flesh, a motion that twisted his middle finger inside her. Static crackled inside her ears, a weightless tickle beginning midthigh. If he didn't stop, this would be over quick. So quick. But that was what she wanted, right? Yes, but she hadn't expected to be overwhelmed so completely. "You're not…last night, you said you w-wouldn't talk like that anymore."

"It doesn't feel like you want me to stop talking, Jas. It feels like just seeing my cock already has you halfway to busting." He scraped his stubble up the side of her neck. "If you'd just crawled into bed with me, I'd have made you sit on it. Bet you would have ridden me hard enough to break the bed. So soaked, you would have slid all over my fucking lap like some kind of dream."

Jasmine's inner walls clenched around his finger with so much power, her head slammed back against the seat. "Oh… oh *no*. Sarge, this is—"

"So bad it's good. So good it's bad." His voice was sharp-edged and sexy beside her ear. "Stop overthinking it, baby, and open your legs to get fingered."

It was easy to do what he said, because he didn't speak like the Sarge of her recollection. This man, this brutal, uncompromising man, was a naughty fantasy come to life, even though compared to the treatment he was inflicting on her body and senses, her fantasies prior to now had been watered-down garbage. She'd never been this hot in her life, never felt the tide between her hips rise so high. If she wasn't careful, it would immerse her…but caution was a presence inside her breastbone, preventing her complete downfall. So yes, *yes*, she opened her legs and felt his thick finger slip deeper, felt the heel of his hand fondle her clit.

"Good," Sarge growled. "Now I'm going to tell you how long you've tortured me with this pretty daydream between your thighs."

He reached across her body and yanked open her hastily thrown-on jacket, before lifting the hem of her T-shirt to expose the puckered breasts straining inside her bra. Jasmine's eyes were closed, but she could practically *feel* his expression shift into one of awe, but that image messed with her head, so she pictured lust instead.

One abrasive palm skated slowly across her cleavage. "I saw you. Changing for bed one night when you probably thought no one was home besides you and my sister." The thrusting of his fingers between her legs picked up speed, as if compelled by whatever his memory was projecting. In deep, out shallow, in deep…again. Again. "I was just walking down the hallway, saw you through a crack in the door. You had on tight purple underwear and no shirt…on your knees going through your overnight bag." She heard him swallow hard. "They were tugged to the side, just a little, so I could see some of your pussy, baby. But it was enough to know I'd never— ever—stop thinking about getting inside of it."

No. *No*, she couldn't be getting increasingly hotter the more he revealed. It was just his hand, just his touch. His wide thumb replaced the grinding heel of his hand, giving her the concentrated pressure she needed to zoom closer to release. "Please, right there. Keep going."

"You think I could stop? I'd sell my fucking soul to watch you come." Jasmine's mouth fell open on a moan when his lips traced over the edge of her bra, his tongue dipping inside and running the length of the material. His breath floated over her, hot and sultry, inspiring goose bumps straight down her body. "Yeah, you were twenty-three when I saw you in those little purple mindfucks." He sucked her nipple through the cotton bra with a lusty sound before releasing it with a quick lick. "You've got some *damn* nerve being twice as hot now, Jas."

That statement alone made the breath pause in her throat, tempted her to finally open her eyes and look at Sarge. But she couldn't—*wouldn't*—look at him while her body reached such an unbelievable peak, or she'd be an addict for life. She was at the base of the mountain now, climbing, climbing, *racing* toward the top, a white-hot clench dropping lower until her hands were clawing at the car door and Sarge's shoulder to keep her corporeal self on the vinyl seat, while the inner being that existed for pleasure alone lifted and bumped along the car's ceiling.

Sarge added a second finger inside Jasmine, and her answering whimper sounded like a different woman. Not her. It couldn't be her. But it was. In that moment, she was a woman who let a man pleasure her inside a car, out in public, and didn't give a thought to the consequences. The only responsibility resting on her shoulders was to *herself.* The cataclysmic need funneling around her, *inside* her, an undeniable force of nature. And *God*, Jasmine wanted to come for Sarge. Wanted to fulfill his fantasy. Create a new one. Right now, inside this car, it didn't feel wrong.

Later, it would, but—

Sarge planted the back of his wrist on the inside of her jeans, wedging his hand and holding his fingers at a slant. "Fuck yourself on my fingers. When you're sliding, riding and bouncing up and down on my dick later, I want to know how those hips look from the side."

With those heated words driving her higher, Jasmine chanced cracking an eyelid to see Sarge's head tilt to the right, to get a better view from the side, licking his upper lip as he looked. His gaze was glassy, fevered, that square jaw tighter than she'd ever seen anyone's. Forcing her eyes back closed before she never wanted to close them again, Jasmine gripped the steering wheel, tweaked her hips back and slid down onto Sarge's large fingers once again. "Shit," she breathed. "Feels so good."

"More," he demanded, his tone dark and rocky. "*More.* Take more, but know that I can fill you so much more with what I've got in my pants."

"Y-*yes*," she said on a stuttered exhale. "I know…I saw."

Jesus, had she really said that out loud? It ceased to matter amid their mutual heavy breathing, the sound of her backside sliding on the seat as she worked up and down his fingers.

Something told her the noises falling from Sarge's mouth would ring in her head for days. Broken, desperate growls, interrupted by rushed pulls of air. Like he was drowning, just like her. "You did see it, didn't you, baby? Saw me all fat and dying to come? I spent the night listening to your tight body roll around on that creaky bed. You've never heard it creak the way it will if I convince you to fuck me." His thumb went into overdrive on her clit, fast and relentless. "But don't worry, baby. I promise no one will hear it over you screaming to get me deeper."

Her bucking hips twisted on his final word, sending a multitude of sensations firing through her blood, seizing her muscles in a locked position to let the pleasure dance on the mountaintop. She wanted to get away, she wanted to get closer, her body didn't know what to do, how to handle the shaking relief. There was even a hint of frustration that she'd only ever been halfway to completion until now, never having been propelled to such a level of fulfilled lust, but it drifted away when she started to come down. It didn't happen all at once, but in softening degrees.

When an iota of mental consciousness became possible, Jasmine heard her own voice repeating "yes, yes, yes," on a throaty loop. Felt Sarge's tongue raking up and down the side of her neck, his teeth taking small bites from her shoulder.

Jasmine no longer kept her eyes closed as a defense mechanism, but because she didn't have the strength to lift her lids. Something jabbed in her throat when she felt Sarge—now kissing across her shoulder—tug her panties back into place and zip her jeans.

"I'm not going to sit here waiting for some big talk to fuck everything up," he gritted out, arousal thick in his tone. "I'm going to go back inside. I'm going to use the same hand that just made you come to jerk myself off. So damn hard. And later? Later, I'm going to hope you come home wanting the real thing from me." He took her hand and squeezed it around what could only be his denim-covered erection. "Baby, we both know the real thing is what I've got."

"You're so arrogant now," she whispered on a huffed breath, unable to put the required exasperation in her voice.

"No, I'm not. I'm overcompensating for the fear that you're going to take one orgasm and run." He sounded almost angry. "You should know I'm going to make doing that really hard for you."

God, why wouldn't her heart stop slamming against her ribs? "Somehow I already knew that."

"Good. Maybe you're finally paying attention where I'm concerned." When his mouth settled at the corner of Jasmine's mouth, she startled, and Sarge sighed. "Be safe at work, will you?"

"Okay," she murmured as he left the car, the door closing with a firm *click* behind his retreating form.

Holy shit. Something told her safety wasn't a concern at work this week. The hazards started and ended with the big compelling man crashing out in her home.

# Chapter Five

For once, Sarge was actually grateful that Lita needed to be bailed out. The Old News drummer had wasted no time since returning from tour to raise some hell, being tossed into Manhattan Central Booking her first night back on a drunk and disorderly charge. While her one phone call should have been to James, Lita had called Sarge's cell phone instead. But if Sarge knew Lita — and you didn't spend years with someone on a tour bus without seeing their worst — she'd called Sarge with the express purpose of getting a rise out of their manager.

Sarge, however, didn't have the desire to go a round with James by not alerting him to Lita's latest antics, so there he stood, after an hour on the train. Outside Central Booking, waiting for James to show up and bail out Lita.

Again.

From his vantage point, he could see three separate Santa Clauses ringing bells for donations to the Salvation Army and wondered why they couldn't at least attempt to appear like the real deal, finding their own damn blocks to work.

*Taking potshots at charities now, are we?* God, he was

in a shitty mood. The back of Sarge's neck itched; his winter clothes felt too tight. Sweat pooled at the base of his spine, even though the temperature sat squarely at thirty-five degrees. And while he wanted Lita's latest stunt to be the reason for his irritable state, it had more to do with her calling from jail before he could…*relieve* himself this morning.

Honestly, he should be *dead* by now. Killed off from an unusual case of purple testicles. He'd slammed back into Jasmine's apartment, all but salivating with the need to take out his *villainous* erection and stroke it to the memory of Jasmine's sexy waist shuddering as she climaxed for his fingers…and his phone had rung. If he hadn't had one fist propped on the entry table while he unzipped his jeans with the opposite hand, he wouldn't even have seen Central Booking pop up on the screen of his phone, where he'd left it by the door. But he had. And he'd known if he missed the call, his pain-in-the-ass bandmate would be shit out of luck.

So with an agonized shout at the ceiling, he'd abandoned his quest for self-love and answered.

Now? He couldn't blink without his dick getting hard.

Jasmine. *God.* The way she'd popped those hips back and slid forward, choking his fingers with her tight—he'd *known* it would be—pussy. The way her lower lip pouted every time he talked dirty in her ear, as if she didn't understand why she liked it so much. At least, he prayed like hell she liked it, because he didn't appear to be capable of keeping the words locked inside, the way he always did until it came time to write songs. Although didn't it make perfect sense that Jasmine would call forward the words, since his songs were about her?

Sarge leaned back against the gray limestone building, mentally berating James for not being his usual early self. He wanted to get back to Hook. Tomorrow night, he would meet his niece for the first time. Spend some clearly much-needed time with his sister. Tonight he would go back to Jasmine's and hope she hadn't already put his possessions on the curb. Oh, and also hope she'd let him fuck the stuffing out of her. He couldn't forget about that.

As if he could. He had a near-decadelong obsession with a woman—no end in sight...*yet*—and a punishing, uncompromising need to get deep, deep inside her where he hoped to lay the obsession to rest. If there was a stern voice in his head telling him on repeat that his heart would be set on fire like Jimi Hendrix's guitar once all was said and done? He was beyond listening. Distance hadn't worked. So he would eliminate every speck of daylight between them and attempt to grind his infatuation into dust.

Sarge pushed off the wall when he saw James approaching, looking as though he wanted to tear down the city with his bare hands. "Hey, man."

"Is she still in holding? Have you gone in yet?"

"Not yet." When James tried to bypass him into the building, Sarge stepped into his path, ceasing his progress with a hand to the chest. "I waited out here for a reason. You need to cool off before you see her."

James shook him off and stepped back, tugging on the sleeves of his trench coat with meticulous movements. "Trust me, I'm feeling positively chilly."

Sarge noticed a photographer across the street taking pictures of them and turned his back, indicating that James should do the same. Not that it would be anything new when gossip blogs broke the news that once again, Lita Regina had ended up behind bars for the night. "It doesn't matter if I trust you. It matters that Lita expects you to go in there and throw your weight around like an asshole. You do it every time." Sarge shook his head. "She loves it."

For once, James actually looked interested in something, one dark eyebrow dipping behind his aviator sunglasses. "Why would she love it?"

"So she can be angry at you instead of herself," Sarge near-shouted, jabbing the freezing air with a finger. "*Shit.* You know what else? I'm done playing referee for you two. You're both reasonably intelligent people—you can figure each other out without my help. I've hit my limit."

James took off his sunglasses with a casual sweep of his hand, removing a square of material from his coat pocket to clean the lenses. When he was finished with the task, he replaced them over his eyes and nodded once at Sarge. "Your sister wasn't quite as enamored by the prodigal son's return as you'd hoped, I take it?"

"Oh, just fuck *right* off." Sarge bypassed James on his way toward the entrance. Yeah, he was well aware that he was taking out his piss-poor mood on James, but someone could ask his rock-hard balls if he cared. Until he got back to Hook and got his own family situation—and the Jasmine situation—under control, he didn't have the capacity to focus on much else.

The two men showed identification and signed in at the glass enclosure just beyond the entrance vestibule. James spoke in a curt tone with the officer as he completed the bail transaction. After funds and paperwork had exchanged hands, they were escorted by a female officer to a beige waiting area where Sarge dropped into an orange plastic seat and James began to pace.

It was a familiar position for them.

Sarge reached over and picked up the nearest magazine from a stack on the wobbly side table, but closed the rag immediately when his face popped up on the fourth page under speculation that the band was breaking up, piggybacked by an article about his recent hookup with a reality show star he'd never met in his life.

Neat.

Sarge realized James had stopped his nervous laps around

the room, and was now standing with his buffed loafers pointing in his direction. "What?"

"I'm waiting to hear what happened with your sister."

"Then it's a good thing you're in a waiting room."

A muscle ticked in the band manager's cheek. "You're not acting like your usual self. Something must have happened, and I'm your manager. So."

Sarge lifted his hands and let them drop to his bent knees. "You just want me to distract you until they release Lita."

"Partly."

Sarge had no choice but to laugh, but it faded fast. He and James got along fine in their silent agreement not to discuss feelings, but in an artistic profession, shit tended to come out in the wash, whether in song lyrics or after a particularly sloppy night out on the road. It didn't matter how succinct he made his explanation, James would see everything. Same way Sarge saw what was taking place between James and Lita. But hell, Sarge needed a distraction from thinking about Jasmine—about everything—so he'd talk. Anything to get him through another ten minutes without wondering what the night would bring.

"My sister didn't want me to stay," Sarge began. "She had a rough breakup with the father of my niece. Doesn't want her daughter to get attached to me since I'll only leave again."

"Right." James sat back in his chair, thumb tapping on his thigh. "Where are you staying?"

Sarge stared hard at the cinder-block wall when he answered. "With Jasmine."

His manager was silent for a tick. "*The* Jasmine? Jasmine *Taveras*?"

Hearing her name felt like rolling around in burning cinders. "I liked you better as guy who doesn't give a shit."

James started to say something else, but the metal door on the opposite side of the room swung open to reveal Lita.

Barely reaching the escorting officer's shoulder, she had both hands shoved into her ripped jeans, a red-and-black-checkered beanie pulled just above huge, apprehensive green eyes, which were firmly trained on James. "Um." She shifted in her boots. "I'm with the band?"

In an effort to keep from pissing off James, since the poor fucker had stopped breathing beside him, Sarge didn't voice the other half of the band's inside joke. Lita's innocent, kid-sister appearance had gotten her stopped at security more than once at Old News shows. She looked incapable of lifting a pair of drumsticks, let alone whaling on a kit like a legend. Once, before a show in Amsterdam, she'd told the venue's head of security she was "with the band," to which he'd replied in a deadpan tone, "The Spice Girls broke up fifteen years ago."

Now, even though Lita wasn't looking at Sarge, he knew she expected the rejoinder, but how the situation was handled needed to be James's call this time. Too often, Sarge had played good cop, and clearly, it hadn't done a damn thing to keep Lita from diving back into self-destructive waters.

Thinking of his fingers thrusting into Jasmine's addictive heat that morning, Sarge wondered if he'd jumped headfirst into self-destruction himself.

Finally, Lita turned her attention to him, arms crossing over her middle. "You were supposed to come alone, Sergeant."

Sarge shrugged, but sighed when he couldn't pull off being callous when it came to Lita, even though she'd used the nickname she knew he couldn't stand. "You were supposed to stay out of trouble."

"Maybe this is just a surprise band reunion and you're both on hidden camera." She elbowed the stone-faced guard to her right. "Smile."

"*Lita*," James started in a warning tone, but when the

drummer's gaze turned hopeful, Sarge could all but feel the shift in his manager's demeanor. "I…uh. Brought you some aspirin."

Lita's expression turned dumbfounded as James approached, producing a bottle of water and aspirin out of his deep coat pockets. When Lita only watched him with suspicion, he lifted her hand, placed the tiny white pills inside, and closed her fist around the medicine. "What are you doing?"

The sound of James clearing his throat bounced off the walls, making it sound louder. "I assume since you drank your weight in whiskey and attempted to scale the Chrysler Building last night, you likely have a headache."

Trying not to be obvious, Sarge patted the air in the universal sign of *take it down a notch, man.* James showed no sign of acknowledgment, but he handed Lita the water bottle. The drummer stared down at it like a foreign object. "Wait. What's going on here? You're supposed to be listing every way I fail at life by now."

James's wince was almost imperceptible. "Yes, well. I'm not going to do that." He took a deep breath and laid a hand on Lita's shoulder, touching her for the first time that Sarge had ever witnessed. "I'm just…I'm glad you weren't hurt."

*And this is why you never give unsolicited advice,* Sarge thought, as Lita tensed, moisture gathering in her widened eyes. James frowned down at the drummer, as baffled by her reaction as Sarge. Maybe four years wasn't enough time to get to know someone, because he certainly didn't expect Lita to haul back and throw the water bottle across the room, where it exploded against the cinder block. No sooner were her hands free than she shoved an unmovable James, backing toward the exit like a terrified cat.

"Look, thanks for bailing me out, but this is where we part ways." Lita split a look between them. "It wasn't a good day to try something new."

James stepped forward, hands fisted at his sides. "Lita — "

"No." She shook her head, warding him off with a hand. "I'm out of here. Stop following me. Stop checking up on me. I don't *need* you."

When the manager only fell into silence, Sarge made a last-ditch effort to calm the drummer by giving her a reassuring smile. "Hey. I hear the Spice Girls broke up fifteen years ago."

"Too little, too late," Lita called as the metal door slammed behind her.

The look James gave Sarge was pure murder as the manager stormed past and went after Lita, leaving Sarge alone in the waiting room with the escorting officer.

"Hey, man. Can I get a picture with you?"

On the upside, his hard-on was only a sweet memory. But something told him it would be back in full effect as soon as he breached the Lincoln Tunnel exit into New Jersey.

• • •

Jasmine sat on the factory roof, her sandwich forgotten on the cinder-block ledge beside her. From her vantage point, she could see Manhattan. And if she closed her eyes really tight and blocked out the mechanical hum from the factory beneath, she could feel the whir of yellow cabs soaring down Broadway. See the white steam curling out of crisscrossed grates midavenue. Hear the new wave of young city dwellers laughing, breathing hot air into their hands as they convened over paper coffee cups.

From the time her parents had moved their family from the Dominican Republic to Hook during high school, she'd pictured herself flitting across the electric backdrop of Manhattan. Reading the newspaper on her balcony, going on outrageous dates just to tell the tale the following morning.

Getting a callback about her demo tape and being whisked away into a life of limousines, parties, and photo shoots.

If you don't dream big, what's the point of dreaming at all? She'd said those exact words countless times. Written them in yearbooks…and yeah, she'd even said them to Sarge. The problem with dreaming, though, was that when it came time to *do*? That's when shit got real. That's when rejection letters—or oftentimes no response at all—started popping the little dream balloons one by one, until the ground at her feet was littered with useless scraps of rubber. Jasmine could still hear the dial tone in her ear, feel her last hope slip away. Not marketable. Not current enough. Not now.

When it had come time to face facts, that her window of opportunity had closed and it was time to start behaving like an adult, Jasmine had bitten the bullet and applied for a position at the factory, much to the quiet disappointment of everyone with whom she'd attended high school. That first day on the assembly line had been a tough pill to swallow. But she'd put her head down, gotten to work…and hadn't lifted it since.

The warning bell pealed, telling workers that lunchtime was ending in ten minutes. Realizing she hadn't even taken a bite of her sandwich, Jasmine made a grab for it, but was distracted when her cell phone rang.

Los Angeles area code? It had to be Sarge. And oh Lord, some very important lady muscles went tight at the prospect of hearing that voice in her ear, right where it had been this morning. With a blown-out breath, she answered. "Hi."

"Hey, Jas." Instead of the gruff, seductive tone she'd been expecting, he sounded out of breath. Stressed. "You busy?"

"I'm on my break." She set the sandwich back down. "Is everything okay?"

He hummed a noncommittal sound, but she could hear booted footsteps moving in the background. "Depends on your definition of okay, I guess."

"I'm going to need you to stop being vague."

His gust of rich laughter hit her ear, making her shiver. "Fair enough. I, uh…" Was he running? "I noticed you didn't have any Christmas decorations up in the apartment, so I stopped on my way back from the city, thinking I'd grab some, right?" More pounding footsteps. "But it turns out someone filmed that little scuffle with your date at the Third Shift last night and it's all over the Web. I've got a few photographers giving me a workout, trying to get a statement. Are you eating lunch?"

During the course of Sarge's explanation, Jasmine had stood up, staring in the direction of Manhattan as if she could pinpoint his location. "You're running away from paparazzi… and asking me about lunch?"

"You left without eating breakfast and I feel responsible."

A hot flutter wound through Jasmine's middle, a secret smile curling her lips. "Are you in need of some assistance, Naughty Prince?"

His growl crawled down the line. "You been looking me up, baby?"

*Good God.* How could be make her stomach dip with a single gruff question? "I'm not *that* far out of the loop," Jasmine murmured. In a small town like Hook, people tended to talk about their homegrown hero. She'd always laughed it off, remembering the young man he'd been, not equating him with the rock god everyone described him as. Now everything about him was coming through a fresh perspective. "And you didn't answer my question."

When he spoke, his voice echoed, as if he'd entered a small space. "Listen, I don't think I can get back on the same train." His heavy sigh tugged something inside her chest. "If you can get out of work, I'm in a Dunkin' Donuts bathroom just out of Newark."

"You're not serious."

"There's Christmas decorations in it for you," he coaxed.

That gave her pause. He was only supposed to spend one night. Now he wanted to decorate with her? Bad idea. *Bad.* On cue, the end-of-lunch bell gave a deafening peal, forcing her to make a call. "I'll tell the floor manager I'm feeling sick," she said, shaking her head. "Don't go anywhere."

"Funny."

# Chapter Six

All right, so being rescued from a Dunkin' Donuts bathroom wasn't Sarge's finest moment. But on the bright side, he was back inside Jasmine's apartment, his possessions were still in the guest room, and he could smell her shampoo through the bathroom door. That's right. Jasmine was taking a shower, mere yards from where he stood untangling a box of Christmas lights. Keeping his hands occupied was a necessity, because if she stayed in the bathroom much longer with the sound of water pelting the tub after rolling off her body, he might have to join her.

After she'd called him from outside the doughnut shop, pushing open the passenger-side door and peeling out of the parking lot the second he dived in, their ride back to Hook had been somewhat tense. From the passenger seat, he'd watched Jasmine brush at grease stains on her coveralls, tugging at her collar, and shifting uncomfortably. If he didn't know Jasmine, he would have thought she was…embarrassed. And not just because the last time they'd been together, he'd had his hand down her pants. No sooner had they walked into the apartment than she was grabbing a change of clothes and shutting herself in the bathroom.

When Jasmine finally emerged, the scent that escaped with her from the bathroom produced a low groan from his throat. She'd thrown on red terry cloth shorts and a tight-fitting white tank top, and the lingering shower steam had molded the material to her tits. Sarge's mouth was devoid of moisture in seconds. Would tonight be the night he worked her out of his conscious? Impossible to tell. She seemed to have thrown up an even bigger wall between them since that morning, but he found himself reluctant to tear it down...with sex. There was a vulnerability to Jasmine now that he would have never equated with her in the past. And there was an answering discomfort in his chest as a result.

Jasmine narrowed her gaze at his feet. Or more accurately, the spindly little pine tree he'd dug up from the median across the street while she'd been in the shower. "What is that?"

"It's your Christmas tree." He considered the greenery, spotting what looked like chewed gum stuck to the bark. "All right, so it's more of a Christmas branch, but I was improvising."

She tapped the hairbrush she held against her thigh. "I didn't...you don't need to do any of this."

"Ah, come on." He picked up the lights again, plugging them into an outlet to make sure they worked. A stall tactic while he figured out how to make her stop looking so defensive. "I haven't decorated for Christmas in years. Humor me?"

All right, sweet. That appeared to work. Jasmine nodded, running the brush through her hair...and making it damn difficult to keep from staring. The red material of her shorts hugged the flesh where he'd buried his fingers only that morning. He needed them there again, but some mysterious intuition told him not to push. Not yet. Sarge laid the lights down on the couch and reached for the Christmas branch, but paused when singing infiltrated the quiet apartment, soft at first, then louder. Voices from outside lifted in harmony together in a familiar Christmas carol that brought a smile to his face.

"The church still sends the choir around, huh?" After a moment, Jasmine nodded. "Let's go out and join them," he said on impulse, holding out a hand for her to take.

"What? No. I can't." She appeared frozen to the spot. "I'm sorry, I can't."

There was actual apprehension in her voice, in her tense demeanor, and it made his hand drop. "I haven't heard you sing once since I got back, Jasmine. I remember when you couldn't go five minutes."

"I don't remember that," said too quickly.

Sarge moved in her direction. "Yes, you do."

"You've called me a liar twice today," she said, warding him off with a hand.

"And I was right both times." He walked right into her touch. "If you talk to me about it, I'll understand."

Her laughter was abrupt and didn't disguise the sadness. "Crowds of people buying tickets to watch you sing, major labels offering you deals...the same labels that closed their door in my face. You couldn't understand, Sarge."

Ouch. "No, but I understand rejection. And there are days I don't want to sing, either, Jasmine. A lot of them." He circled her wrist and pulled her close, willing her to look up at him, which she finally did. "Come on, baby. Let's go show them how it's done."

Sarge held his breath as—for just a split second—she looked to be considering whether to go outside, chewing her lip in a distracting way. He was watching her so closely, he saw fear. Fear that flickered into something else. Intention. Maybe a hint of self-preservation, too. It should have prepared him for what came next, but nothing could have. Nothing ever would. Jasmine sidled close, letting her curves brush over him…and then she hit him with a heavy-lidded look that called to mind sweaty, middle-of-the-night sex. She picked up his hand and slid it beneath her tank top, stopping just beneath her tits, then guiding it over one pointed mound oh so slowly. "I'd rather stay inside where it's warm, wouldn't you?"

He was caught midgroan when she nudged him backward. The backs of his legs hit the couch and he went down onto the cushions, Jasmine wasting no time straddling his lap. Jesus. This is what he'd wanted. A way out of his obsession. A way to break the curse. But even as lust raced through him, common sense reared its head. Common sense and the fact that he cared about her, no matter the torture she'd put him through. *It's a tactic. Don't go down without a fight.* "I know you're just trying to distract me." Sarge tried to avoid looking at the gorgeous mouth hovering so close. Lost the battle. "Ahhh. You'd really seduce me just to avoid singing? How bad is it, Jas?"

"Stop." Jasmine slid her fingers into his hair, brought their mouths against each other. "Please, stop?"

It was like being under hypnosis. Not just his mind, but his body. The woman who ruled both had said *please* and stolen his willpower. His dick swelled, enthusiastic to make contact with the entrance to her body, even through their clothes. His hands itched to throw her down on the couch and punish her for ruining him. For everything. For every*one*. But he could feel the hurt inside her, and digging it up at the root needed to take precedent. "Talk to me, baby. Where did your voice go?"

"No one wants to hear it," she breathed against his mouth.

"I do." Kissing her mouth was a temptation he couldn't turn down, but he pulled back after only one wet meshing of lips. *God,* her taste. "I can hear you in my head right now. I've never forgotten—"

Jasmine shot forward and captured his mouth, the kiss desperate. Sarge growled when their tongues met, testosterone gripping him below the belt. There was a warning in the back of his mind, reminding him Jasmine was only avoiding a conversation, but his body felt only the pull of need radiating from her. Physical need. It called to his own and swamped his good intentions. "Tell me now where you want this to go," he rasped, drawing on her bottom lip. "If we're going to fuck, I need to blow off some steam first. You've had my cock hard since this morning, and I'm already right on the edge."

Her fingers flexed on his shoulders, digging into muscle. "I don't…I'm not ready to go there yet." She spread her knees wider on the couch, rubbing herself against his bulge with a whimper. "But w-we shouldn't be doing this, Sar—"

Sarge interrupted her with an openmouthed kiss, an aggressive one that bent her backward over his thighs. "Got it, baby. No fucking." He hooked his fingers under the hem of her tank top. "You going to let me see your tits, though, Jas? Going to let me have a suck of those tips?" Through the material of her tank, he licked over one pointed peak. "If you let me take this tank top off, I can fuck you without taking out my cock."

The words were barely out of his mouth when Jasmine whipped the white material over her head, tossing it beside them on the couch. Sarge almost went off in his jeans. Jesus. *Jesus*. His youth had been filled with prayers that those breasts would spill out of her bathing suit top, but seeing them up close and personal blew his fantasy to hell. "Gorgeous," he managed. "They're…*you* are gorgeous."

Why did she look surprised? As if no one had told her in a while. "Show me."

Sarge gripped Jasmine's ass and yanked her close, swallowing a groan at the new positioning of his cock, wedged between her pussy and his stomach. Hunger to taste had him salivating, licking his lips as he leaned in to draw on her nipples. When Sarge finally got there, finally suctioned his lips around one straining, rose-tinted bud, the hunger turned desperate. The unfulfilled needs of his past packed themselves into a right hook, knocking out present Sarge, leaving only the starved, frustrated young man he'd been those years ago. He wasn't gentle about drawing Jasmine close, so close she was grinding down on his hard dick just by breathing. His mouth slipped from one breast to the other, his parted lips dragging through the valley between with panting breaths. "Kept them from me. You kept them from me. I just wanted to see...*needed* to see..."

Jasmine's fingers shook as they transferred from his shoulders to his hair, fingernails raking along his scalp. His grip on her ass gained strength, rocking his body like a ship in a storm, jerking her up and down on his erection. Although "erection" was a weak word for his entire body hovering on the brink of goddamn insanity. Jasmine. He was sucking Jasmine's tits and his body could barely stand the inferno he'd been plunged into.

"Sarge. Please, I...*oh God*." Her thighs strained from their spread position on his lap, inched a touch wider. "If y-you keep doing that, I'm going to—"

"*Good*." He all but roared the word against her shiny nipple and felt a shiver pass through her undulating body. "Ride me, use me, come on me. God knows I've used the thought of you to come for a fucking decade."

Sarge grated the last word with his mouth around her nipple, then hollowed his cheeks getting that sweet peak sucked good and hard. Somewhere in the back of his head, he knew his hold on her ass would leave bruises, but stopping the torment of Jasmine dry-humping him through their clothes would be far worse torture. When she climaxed, Jasmine shook like a leaf, breathy, fragmented words bursting free on gusts of breath. "Oh *God*…you're…oh it's…so good."

Sarge watched her in awe while lapping at her nipples. One, then the other. "Want another, baby?"

Really, he was in no position to be offering her a second orgasm. The head of his cock was wet with precome, probably visible against the front of his pants. Tremors were rocking through his thighs and stomach with the urge to fuck. To pin her down, plow himself deep, and pump like a nasty dog. This had started as a way to take the fear out of her eyes, hadn't it? *Jesus*. He could barely think through the desire eating him alive. Still, if she needed more, he would find a way to hold back.

Sarge leaned in to kiss her mouth, a long, groaning kiss as his hand landed on her backside with a light slap. "You need more? Go get it, Jas. Let's see how wet we can get that little red strip of shorts guarding your pussy."

"No," Jasmine gasped, pushing him back against the couch, her hips beginning a slow bucking motion, like a dancer in a music video. "You already gave me more. This morning… and now. But you haven't — "

"You're not making me come in my jeans, Jasmine." He almost choked on the male pride that clouded up his throat. The obnoxious buzz of embarrassment left over from his teenage years. "Not now. Not as a man."

"Yes." Determination flared in Jasmine's expression, and then there was nothing but the repeated stroking friction from the base of his cock up…back down…

"*Stop*," he groaned, his hands contradicting the command by sliding down the back of her shorts to encounter the bare flesh of her ass, punishing it with a kneading massage. "You can't do this to me again."

Oh fuck, he wasn't going to make it. The more extreme his mental agony became, the faster she whipped her hips up and back, her open mouth dragging over his with every movement. "Sarge," she moaned. "You feel so good. So huge."

Call him a cliché, but that was his point of no return. Hearing the woman that haunted his fantasies refer to his cock as *huge* robbed his balls of their weight, sending moisture from deep, deep down in the root of him to dampen the lap of his jeans. His throat was scraped raw from saying her name, but he couldn't remember having said it once. Never had he been so satisfied from an orgasm and he knew, *knew* it was Jasmine, the woman watching him in amazement from her perch on his thighs. Maybe later he would interpret that expression differently, but not right now. *Now* he only saw his tormentor delighted by how much control she had over his body. How much control she'd *always* had over it.

And he'd just busted in his pants as if he hadn't aged a goddamn day.

"That makes you happy, doesn't it?" He invaded her personal space, bringing their faces close. "Knowing how easily you can get me off?"

"Yeah," she whispered, scrutinizing his face. "It kind of does."

Anger—directed at his past and current self, and at Jasmine—spit hot lava against the inside of his gut. He had to get out of there. Clean himself off. Play his guitar. Something. *Anything* but having Jasmine looking at him like some exotic specimen she'd never encountered.

He picked Jasmine up by the hips and set her aside on the couch. "I'm going to turn in," he said, hating the curtness in his voice, but too embarrassed to change it. "Thanks for not putting my stuff on the curb, all right?"

He was already at the guest room door when she spoke. "Sarge—"

The door closed before she could continue. No way would he sit there and listen to Jasmine try to convince him his reaction was natural. Normal. It wasn't.

And instead of doing something to rid himself of the curse, every encounter with Jasmine only seemed to increase its potency. Tomorrow. Tomorrow he would regroup.

His sanity depended on it.

• • •

Jasmine kept it real. If you interviewed the Taveras family, they would tell you she told the truth and didn't smother it in sugar. It wasn't just a matter of telling people when their new haircut looked a mess or they were acting a damn fool. It was more than that. She owned up to her mistakes and felt no qualms with admitting her error in judgment.

Once during senior year of high school, she'd accidentally burned off a hunk of River's hair with a curling iron, and instead of trying to hide it or simply apologizing, she'd snipped off an equal piece of her own, so they could match. Just one month ago, she'd clipped another shopper's car bumper at the mall and waited outside for an hour until the person emerged. And okay, her tenacity had somewhat stemmed from the hope they could trade cash instead of going through their insurance companies. New Jersey rates were no joke.

Point being, since Sarge had shown back up in Hook, she'd been running in a mistake marathon. Really delicious, pulse-pounding, unforgettable, ooey-gooey mistakes. With her best friend's little — okay, maybe not so little at all — brother, a man seven years her junior. Who even did that? Everyone knew it was only hot the other way around. When a guy hooked up with his best friend's little sister after being tempted into a near coma. Who didn't get a little hot thinking about *that*? But this? This was veritable cradle robbery of a guy she'd once been paid to supervise during his adolescence. Worse, it had been done behind River's back. Her best friend on the planet.

Junior year of high school, when Jasmine had moved to

this über-Irish and Italian town, her Dominican heritage had stuck out like ten sore thumbs. Every guy had wanted to date her, in a way that told Jasmine they viewed her as a novelty. There had been no love lost when she'd turned them all down, especially from the girls at school who thought her stuck up. River Purcell had been the last person Jasmine expected to approach her. Freshman class president, head cheerleader, gorgeous in a way that made passersby shake their heads. River had had everything going for her. But she'd sat down right beside Jasmine where she'd been eating outside the gymnasium and they'd never gone a day without speaking since, even after Jasmine graduated from high school and River still had two years left.

Jasmine massaged the back of her neck in the break room, attempting to psyche herself up for the upcoming confrontation with her best friend. This is what she did. She fessed up when she did something wrong.

*That makes you happy, doesn't it? Knowing how easily you can get me off?*

*Dios*, "liked" didn't begin to cover how satisfying Sarge's body had made her feel last night. Powerful. Buoyant. Feelings she hadn't encountered in so long.

What if she wasn't ready to give him up just yet?

Even considering a second time was so, so wrong on *more* than one level. Usually when she made a mistake, she regretted it and swore she'd never do it again. But each time Jasmine spoke the promise out loud—as practice for the real deal—the words got stuck in her throat. Perhaps it was her body banding together to keep the promise suppressed, each little part playing its own role. Her nipples were the ringleaders, tightened to the point of pain inside her factory jumpsuit. Stemming from those pesky peaks was a bobbing line twisting its way down to her tummy, twirling there like a horny, demented ballerina.

Jasmine's palms pressed against her cheeks to cool them down, but they only glowed hotter beneath her touch. With each tick toward the workday's closing bell, her body prepared a little more. Preparing for going home and finding Sarge in her apartment, perhaps still a little angry at her for pushing him past his breaking point last night. Needing to prove something. She'd caught herself pressing her stomach against her station this morning, just for the anchor of contact. Her thighs wouldn't stop rubbing together, the resulting chafe burning her up with fever. No denying it, she wanted a second helping. Wanted those hands on her again, that bulge pressing between her legs. Wanted that rock star voice in her ear.

She was clearly a sick individual.

River stuck her head into the break room, a pink bubble popping between her lips. "Break's over. You coming?"

"Yeah. Yes."

Jasmine retrieved her safety goggles and hard hat from the ancient break table and followed her friend onto the noisy factory floor. They passed familiar faces that smiled absently as they passed, their focus already back on the work. The factory didn't produce one single product. It pumped out various items, such as display stands and cheap camera tripods for numerous retailers. Their number one contract, however, was from the Motor Vehicle Commission for license plates, which made the factory walls feel more like a prison than its soot-stained gray interior and the hard-assed supervisors that roamed the assembly lines. But the workers were family— each and every one of them. They covered for one another when necessary and picked up slack when someone wasn't feeling up to snuff.

River and Jasmine didn't always get to work side by side, but today they'd been placed in the same production cluster. They moved in a concentrated rhythm, River retrieving the blank plate and consulting the order sheet, before Jasmine used the heavy machinery to stamp the plate with its respective number.

Jasmine lifted a finished plate and placed it on the conveyor belt, adjacent to her workstation. "So…" she started, feeling seasick. "Your brother and—"

"Oh my *God*," River interjected, speaking loudly to be heard over the clanging metal around them. "Didn't he get *huge*?"

A vision of Sarge sprawled out on her guest bed, thrusting his erection into his own hand, swamped her, intensifying her seasickness like a tidal wave beneath a ship. "Yes. That's a… fact."

"I mean, remember when we were in high school? Never lifted his head from that guitar, just strumming and brooding, strumming and brooding, all day long."

Jasmine swallowed the dust coating her throat. "I remember." Only, since last night, she'd kind of been wondering if she'd been *mis*remembering all this time. Until he'd returned home, when she thought of Sarge, she saw him in her mind's eye stewing down at his guitar. But now? Now she had the overwhelming feeling he'd been looking at, well… *her.* "He's definitely changed."

River squinted at the order sheet, running her index finger down the stuffed clipboard. "I haven't slept since sending him away. I'm sure you've been making him comfortable, though."

*Ay, Dios.* "Something like that."

"What does that mean?" River murmured, still focused on the clipboard.

Jasmine heaved in a deep breath. "It means, he—we—there was…physical contact. Of the biblical variety. Like, we're not in Revelations yet, but we're moving pretty quickly through the Old Testament." And oh man, the impact of what she'd done hadn't fully registered until River's blue eyes went wide enough to damn near swallow her face. Jasmine rushed to release more words, just to delay whatever River's response would be. "He just kept coming at me, Riv. I...he's nothing like the Sarge I remember. One minute he was, like, hey, eat this sandwich, and then there were no clothes. Just *none*."

River tossed the paperwork onto a nearby folding chair. "You hooked up with my brother?" She sounded dazed. "He's twenty-two."

"I know." Jasmine smacked a gloved hand over her face. "What is a suitable punishment here? Public humiliation? Should I wear a sandwich board outside the factory tonight?"

River folder her arms. "That depends. What would it say?"

Jasmine let the glove covering her face drop. "Women of Hook: lock up your sons?"

When a laugh burst from her best friend's mouth, Jasmine's jaw dropped. "Are you *laughing* right now?"

"Yes, and it feels pretty damn good." River's shoulders lifted on a deep breath. "I keep waiting for you to say it was a onetime thing. But you haven't."

"It was a..."

River lifted an eyebrow.

"Onetime..."

This time, her best friend doubled over laughing, drawing the attention of the supervisor. Trading a glance, they picked up working where they'd left off. They worked without talking until the dour-faced supervisor had moved on to the next row before River spoke. "Look. You're both adults. It's none of my business."

"Oh, come on." Jasmine frowned. "Don't be understanding. That's so much worse than anger or ridicule."

River was silent a moment, her amused expression transforming to one she'd been wearing a lot lately. Worried, pensive, downtrodden. "Jas, you're the smartest person I know, so you've already thought about him leaving. Going back out on the road or heading back to L.A. and recording a new album."

Okay, so she hadn't thought about that, but it wasn't an issue. There was no relationship on the table with Sarge. Not even close. She could *never* make another person feel obligated to stay behind in Hook, the way she'd done. Not when they'd already gotten out and had the means to go even further. A rock star shacking up with his factory worker girlfriend in New Jersey. The idea was laughable.

"I know what it feels like when a man leaves." River hit her with a poignant look. "I'm not comparing Sarge to...*him*. But my brother isn't hanging around, either. That's why he's not staying at my house."

A crank twisted in Jasmine's chest, remembering how low River had been brought by her high school sweetheart–turned–Army soldier bailing, leaving her pregnant and brokenhearted. "I understand why you're concerned after everything that happened, Riv. I do. That's not going to happen here." Jasmine pulled the machine's lever down to stamp a blank plate. "You know me. My eyes are open. I'm keeping the right distance, just like I always do."

River regarded her a moment. "Okay, I believe you," she said simply, the downturned corners of her lips popping up into a smile. "So I guess Christmas came early for you this year, huh? Does sending my brother to stay in your guest room count as my gift?"

Jasmine groaned up at the ceiling. "Okay, there's a line and we're totally crossing it into wrongness right now."

"*You* crossed the line," River returned. "I'm just joining you. Pass the salt."

Jasmine treated River to a light hip check. "You're the best."

"I won't argue with that," River said, peeking over from beneath her eyelashes. "Just be careful. I've already got the scorned-woman market cornered in this friendship."

They went back to working with methodical efficiency, passing a gym towel back and forth between them when the machinery made them sweat. For once, Jasmine was grateful to have work as a distraction, although it wasn't blocking her most pressing thoughts. River's warning clanged in her head along with the pumping metal. She'd only spent one night—and one sweltering morning—with new, grown-up Sarge, but it had been enough to know one thing. He was head and shoulders above the men she typically dated. She would need to keep her *own* head on straight, keep their relationship limited to physical pleasure.

In some crazy fantasy world, what would happen if either of them wanted more? Answer: nothing. He was too young to settle down with one woman, especially when hordes of them awaited him on the road. No. The next few days would scratch the big old itch incurred by her upcoming milestone birthday. The three-oh hung over her head, making her anxious to prove she could still attract a younger man. Satisfy him. Make him come back for more.

That's all this was.

# Chapter Seven

Sarge tapped the jewelry case against his thigh as he approached River's house. Did three-year-olds even wear necklaces? The guy at the local jewelry store had seemed positive on that front, but then again, maybe he'd just wanted to make the sale. Guess he'd find out.

The sounds of running feet and squeals of laughter stopped Sarge short halfway up the stoop. He'd never heard those noises coming from inside his childhood home. His parents had both been only children, limiting them to a foursome. Not to mention, his and River's father had been fairly strict, especially when it came to River, who'd shown a high aptitude for schoolwork at an early age. Most of their evenings had been about studying, Sarge sneaking his guitar down to the basement or into the garage whenever he could manage. The sound of a child's laughter was really nice. Nice shouldn't make his stomach sink, though. Should it? It shouldn't make him feel like an intruder. Or someone who'd been in a coma for four years, only to wake up and find a chunk missing from his life.

He shoved the necklace into the back pocket of his jeans, rubbing his damp palm along the leg on its way back around. His nerves were strung tight, even worse than the night Old News played their first gig in Pasadena. Five people had shown up, and one had been James. To this day, however, he swore playing in front of a handful of people was twice the head wreck as a sold-out stadium full. Now it appeared a three-year-old would rattle him far worse than either situation.

Before he could reach the door, the painted white wood swung open and—

Jasmine stepped out.

It was like he'd been storing a shaken bottle of lust in his stomach all day, and someone had just uncapped it, lusty fizz shooting out in every direction. *Christ.* In leggings that molded her thighs and a thin sweater that hugged her tits, he was starving for her in an instant. He hadn't seen her since last night's couch debacle and had spent a good part of the day cursing her name, but now? Now he just wanted another shot. And he wanted it bad. Common sense continued to intrude, telling him it wasn't Jasmine's fault that he'd been consumed by her half his life, but everything below his brain ignored that sentiment, only wanting to get even.

Before Sarge could get a handle on the desire she'd liberated, she spoke in a low voice. "I was going to leave before you got here. Riv just needed someone to keep an eye on Marcy while she cooked. I—"

"Why would you leave?" When Jasmine shivered from the cold, Sarge whipped off his coat with a curse and wrapped it around her shoulders. For the life of him, he couldn't keep his hands from lingering on her arms once he'd transferred the coat, couldn't stop himself from pulling her close. Closer. Their white billows of breath met and danced between them. At once, it felt as though another four years had passed since the last time he'd seen her, rather than a day. Her eyes were flitting around, landing on everything but him, so he grasped her face to hold her still long enough to make eye contact. "Please stay."

"I told your sister what's been happening."

*Jesus.* He didn't know if he should be horrified or glad their encounters had been enough of an event for Jasmine that she'd felt the need to share. "Okay. That might make things a little weird, but I've lived on a bus with musicians. Weird is my new normal."

She gave him that lip-pursing smile that tilted her eyes. "An example, please."

"Our bass player saves his toenails in a coffee can for good luck."

Jasmine whistled low beneath her breath. "Good one."

"Yeah? It never upended in your bunk." It felt so good holding her face and watching her smile gain momentum. He could have stood there the rest of his life and it wouldn't have gotten old. "Come inside. Don't leave because of the weird."

She cast a sidelong look at the house. "Maybe for a little while."

"That'll work until I can get a better answer." Sarge let his thumb trace over her temple, down to her jawline, memorizing the awareness that crept over both of them, breath by breath. The way her stomach went concave against his belt buckle, then shuddered back out. After making sure no one from the house was watching through the window, he dropped both hands and settled them low on her hips, the contact hidden by the sides of his jacket. "You going to let me make you feel good again, Jas?"

Doubt trickled into her expression. "I don't know yet."

"Good. I'm kind of enjoying the convincing process." Sarge coasted a hand over her waistline, flattening it at the small of her back, just above the flare of her ass. "And you ain't seen nothing yet."

"Yeah?" Did he imagine the way she arched and tempted his hand lower? "That's what I'm afraid of."

He nudged her forehead with his own. "I'm the last person you should be afraid of, baby."

"*You* were the baby," she breathed.

"You're overthinking again. Remember what happens when you do that?"

She did an inward roll of her lips and let them pop back out, juicer than before. "You make me stop thinking?"

"That's right." Fuck it. He was going to kiss her. Right there, in the light, on the pathway to his sister's house. That mouth was his. He couldn't *stand* living in a world where he hadn't kissed her yet. They were so close he could feel her minty breath ghosting over his lips and he knew it wouldn't be gentle. She was about to get the kind of kiss that would get her legs up around his waist like a fucking clamp. It was a bad idea right now. Yeah, it really was. But sometimes good things came from the worst ideas, right? "I hope you're okay with being wet at the dinner table."

He yanked her closer—

"*Sarge*," River called from the porch. "Jasmine isn't the main course."

With a sigh brimming with frustration, Sarge dropped his chin onto Jasmine's head. "Forget what I said. Weird is overrated."

When Jasmine backed away, he wrestled with the urge to hang on, but common sense descended, forcing him to follow her up the path. "Hey Riv," he called over Jasmine's head.

His sister twisted a dish towel in her hands. "Well, it's been over a decade, but I finally paid you back for interrupting my first kiss with Vaughn." Both he and Jasmine drew up short at the mention of her ex's name, but River waved the towel at them. "Don't look at me like that. I can say his name out loud, can't I? Anyway, nothing can ruin my mood tonight. I get to have dinner with my two favorite people. Even though they were getting ready to make out on my walkway."

Jasmine turned to him with a raised eyebrow. "See, you get to leave and avoid the jokes. I have to stay and live with them."

Sarge laughed, but the sound was void of any actual humor. Thankfully, neither Jasmine nor River seemed to notice as they entered the house. Jasmine's quip had been a nice little reminder that she would be just peachy once he left. No pining on her end. Just *his*, as always.

Unless he did something about it.

His dark thoughts were obliterated when a tiny blond fairy sprinted across his line of vision, before skidding to a halt and falling with a plop onto her butt. At first, he couldn't see her face because the tumble had loosened her ponytail and covered her face with hair. Hands covered in paint scrambled to push it out of her eyes. Eyes that locked on him like big blue spotlights. Sarge felt his heart grow about fifteen damn sizes inside his chest…

"Mommy, who's that man?"

…and then it up and shattered all over the floor like a glass balloon.

River helped her daughter stand. "Remember, Marcy? I told you Uncle Sarge was coming over to eat dinner at our house. Uncle Sarge is Mommy's brother."

Her tiny nose wrinkled. "Celia's brother is little. Why is yours big?"

"Celia is her friend from school," River explained before kneeling down beside her daughter. "Sarge is much older than Celia's little brother. Someday her little brother will grow up, too."

Marcy gave Sarge a once-over. "Can I hold this one in a blanket?"

The two women covered their mouths to hold in laughter,

but Sarge had no such problem. He was too fascinated by the miniature version of his sister to consider laughing. When he realized the silence had gone on too long and everyone was staring at him, he shook himself. "I have a thing. A, uh... thing." He swiped the jewelry case out of his back pocket, held it awkwardly for a few seconds, before holding it out to Marcy.

After looking up at River for permission, Marcy took a few steps closer, snatched the box, and retreated just as fast. He expected a little girl's prerogative to be to rip off the paper as fast as possible and ask questions later, but she turned it over in her hands, inspecting it like a diamond appraiser. Sarge felt Jasmine watching him and turned to catch her eye, but she snapped her attention back to Marcy before he got a fix. The wrapping paper hit the floor a moment later, and after a small struggle, Marcy pried open the box with River's help.

*Oh Lord. I'm a goner.* Marcy beamed up at him through a gap in her wispy strands of straw-colored hair, and regret that he'd missed the first three years of her life smacked him in the face. Had anything he'd done on the road been worth it?

Marcy tried to fit the necklace over her head without unfastening it, grunting when it got stuck above her nose. "You're better than Celia's brother, I think."

When River nudged him in the shoulder, Sarge realized he was smiling like a goofball, but it vanished when he saw tears in his sister's eyes. "Come on, you necklace-giving jerk." She sniffed, taking his elbow and leading him out of the entryway. "Dinner's ready."

For Sarge, meals were usually unceremonious. Grab a sandwich between recording sessions, stealing a slice of pizza from whoever had taken the trouble to order food. Old News had an unspoken rule that food was a communal entity. Unless it came to James's ever-present box of Triscuits, then God help the poor soul whose hand breached the opening. Sarge had learned that lesson the hard way.

Dinner with three women—okay, two and a half—was an entirely different affair. They took their time, actually breathing between bites, not even arguing over the last dinner roll. Sarge started to protest when River dumped a third helping of mashed potatoes onto his plate, but stopped himself. The more he ate, the happier his sister seemed to get, so he kept packing it away. Until he saw River and Jasmine exchange a covert glance, their amusement obvious.

"Oh, I see. This is some kind of conspiracy." He dropped his fork with a clatter onto the plate and collapsed back in the chair. "I guess there are worse ways to go than overdosing on mashed potatoes."

River burst out laughing. "It wasn't premeditated, but you just kept *going*."

"Who are we to question that kind of dedication?" Jasmine said, smiling into her Diet Coke. "It was like you were competing in a contest against yourself. We hereby declare you the winner."

"You even got Marcy to sit still for a whole meal." River nodded at her giggling daughter. "I think she's in shock."

"Marcy," Sarge groaned. "Tell them to stop teasing me."

The little phenom responded by sliding off her chair and rounding the table to climb onto Sarge's knee. Her elbow dug into his stomach, upsetting the food mountain residing there, but the discomfort was worth it. River brought out dessert a few minutes later. Sarge only managed a bite before tapping out, content to watch Marcy get more chocolate cake on her face than into her stomach. By the time she was finished, her eyes were half closed, head lolling to the side in obvious exhaustion. It was the best dinner Sarge ever had.

"Jas, can you get Marcy's teeth brushed and put her in bed?" River stood and began clearing the table. "I'm going to get these into the dishwasher."

"You got it." When Jasmine stood beside Sarge's chair,

he handed over the sleepy child, his throat aching when they had to pry her fingers from around his shirt collar. Something passed between him and Jasmine when their eyes met, but he had no idea what it was. Or what it meant. He only knew everything about the moment felt good. Felt right. And he wanted to do it all over again tomorrow.

There was no stopping his watching every step Jasmine took up the stairs, carrying his niece on her hip, but as soon as she disappeared upstairs, Sarge went to help River in the kitchen.

"So listen…" she started, covering leftovers and storing them in the fridge. "I know it's short notice and probably a lot to ask—"

"What is it?"

River leaned back against the counter. "There's a church service at Holy Cross on Christmas Eve. I helped organize the potluck dinner afterward at the school gymnasium across the street, and…" She tucked a stray hair behind her ear. "Would you bring your guitar and play a song or two?"

Sarge's eyebrows damn near hit the ceiling. "My songs aren't exactly church-friendly, Riv."

"I know." Pink stained her cheeks. "You could sing a Christmas song, though. You know. Instead of a sex one."

"A sex one." He shook his head. "I thought I knew the meaning of weird. Until tonight."

His sister snapped the dish towel and caught him in the thigh. "Just think about it, okay? You're one of the lucky ones that made it out of Hook. It makes you kind of a big deal." She turned back to the sink. "Now, go kiss your newest admirer good-night. And I'm not talking about Jasmine."

"Right." Rubbing the back of his neck, Sarge pushed through the swinging door of the kitchen and ascended the stairs. He reached the landing just in time to catch Jasmine walking out of Marcy's room, index finger over her lips with a warning to stay quiet. His flare of disappointment over missing his chance to say good-night to Marcy was eclipsed by a righteous punch of hunger when Jasmine hesitated in front of him. As if she wanted to head back downstairs where it was safe, but couldn't quite ignore their being alone again. Not about to let that hesitation go unrewarded, Sarge nudged her back against the hallway wall, gratified as hell when her mouth fell open in a husky pant.

"Not here."

Sarge wondered if she was aware of her hands fisting in his T-shirt, yanking him closer. "Where, baby?" he muttered against the top of her head. "You want to pull the car over a block from here and mount me on the passenger seat? Or wait until we're somewhere I can spread you out and eat you first?"

"*Dios.* I don't know," she breathed, making him pull back to scrutinize her face. She raked her teeth over that pouty lower lip, stiffening his cock. "We just had dinner with your sister, and, well…it reminded me that you're too young for me, Sarge."

"Why can't my being younger work to our advantage?" Sarge asked, tugging her away from the wall, sliding a palm down her rounded backside. He gave the taut flesh a firm squeeze, lifting her up and against him, groaning at the back of his throat when the vee of her thighs notched over his rising erection. *Sweet fuck.* Her leggings made her as good as naked in this position, allowing him to feel the separation of female flesh, the smooth skin on either side. He hadn't been this horny since…that morning. Then again outside on the walkway. How much more of this could he take before ripping her mother-loving clothes off, not a damn given to their surroundings?

What had they been talking about? Right. The advantages of him being seven years younger. This was so not the discussion to have upstairs at his sister's house, but he had Jasmine's attention and he wouldn't waste it.

Sarge transferred his other hand to her ass so both of them were gripping the swell of her cheeks, massaging them slowly. "Yeah, I'm younger. That means I'll need you more often. I probably won't let you out of bed in the morning until you're covered in sweat." When her head tipped back on an uneven exhale, he ran his tongue up her sweet-smelling neck, not even attempting to be neat. He wanted to leave a trail, wanted to know it was there. "I can fill you full of thick dick every time you need to orgasm. Can make it last until you've had enough and your fucking legs start to cramp around my waist."

"Leg cramps shouldn't sound so good," she whispered, slipping a hand beneath his shirt and tracing devastating patterns over his abs. He felt every single one of them below his belt, as if she were jacking him off instead of touching his stomach. *Goddamn*, his cock felt heavy and abused in his jeans, reminding him of that sweltering summer his last year in Hook when he couldn't take two steps without seeing Jasmine in a tight dress or a bathing suit.

"I'm young enough to learn new tricks, too, baby. Learn what makes you scream the loudest, come the hardest, and brings you back for a second, third, and fourth helping."

Finally, *finally*, their lips slid together and his knees almost liquefied from the force of his need, so he tightened his legs and shoved up between her thighs. "I want to fuck you like a beast in heat, Jasmine. And you're wiggling around on top of my cock like you want it bad. So tell me again why my age is a problem."

She answered him in the form of a French kiss, her tongue sliding into his partially open mouth and dragging an agonized groan from his throat. He didn't remember backing Jasmine toward the opposite wall, but suddenly she was flattened by his body on the hard surface while their mouths mated. If someone gave him the choice of a juicy orange or Jasmine's mouth after a week without sustenance, he would have stomped on the orange and gone after her like a starving caveman.

Her fingers twined in his hair, that mindfuck body humping his lap with the small amount of movement their position allowed. Somewhere in the back of his mind, Sarge knew he needed to pull back and wait for the right time. Like when they weren't five feet from his niece's room and a few climbed stairs from his sister discovering them. But Jasmine was purring in her throat and hooking her right leg over his hip to get more cock between her thighs and—

"Oh, shit. Okay," Jasmine panted, breaking away on a strangled moan. "We have to stop."

"I know." Sarge gave a slow roll of his hips, his breathing rough against her swollen mouth. "So quit trying to get me inside you through my jeans and I'll stop."

The sound that escaped her was half laugh, half sob. "This is crazy."

"No." He licked her upper lip, snagged it with his teeth. "Crazy would be staying away from each other because I'm a little younger."

"We need, like…parameters. Or something."

"Fine." With a mighty will, Sarge eased back and let her slip down the wall. "You've got the car ride home to decide what they are."

And Sarge had the ride home to remind himself of his *own* parameters. He could let his body sink in and take, but his head needed to stay above water. He needed to remember what the hell of unsatisfied need felt like—and remember who'd been responsible for putting him there. Tonight he would finally break free.

Why did his own assurance sound so unconvincing?

# Chapter Eight

Jasmine watched Sarge's denim-hugged thighs move as he climbed the stairs to her apartment, a few yards in front of her. She'd insisted he go first, knowing if she felt him staring at her backside with all that brooding concentration, she'd turn around and hurtle herself right toward his sexy bulk, crying *take me, take me, please.* Like some kind of demented, sex-starved meteor from Planet Horny.

*Parameters, parameters…*

Whose idea had that been? Hers. Yes! It was a damn good idea, too, because bad things were afoot. Very bad things, indeed. She'd been feeling Sarge on a physical level since he'd shown up and mowed down Carmine at the Third Shift. Since he'd boosted her up on the kitchen counter like she weighed less than a flea and proceeded to dirty talk her panties into a twist. Tonight, though, things had…shifted. Sarge had all those qualities she remembered. He was perceptive when it came to people's feelings, especially his sister. He could laugh at himself. Facets of a man's personality Jasmine had assumed couldn't be maintained when being showered with all-out fan worship.

Sarge had not only maintained those qualities, he'd turned into an entirely different monster. One that had the nerve to show up with the perfect princess necklace and look like he'd just been hit with a cement truck upon meeting his niece.

What an asshole.

Because now the situation had graduated from wanting to jump Sarge's bones to being interested in what went on behind those blue eyes. Why had he left Hook so abruptly four years ago? What had prompted his return?

Did he sleep with tons of groupies?

*Do not ask. Do not even think of* maybe *asking that.*

She shouldn't care. Sarge's bedroom activities before and after *they* slept together—of which she was still debating the wisdom—should be a nonissue. However, while it was on her mind...*of course* he slept with tons of girls on the road. He was a veritable rock star with almost irritatingly good looks. All of his female admirers were probably a shit-ton younger than her, too. How would she stack up to them?

Jasmine tugged her apartment keys out of her purse, striving for nonchalance even though Sarge had an elbow propped on the doorframe, watching her like a dragon from the shadows.

"What?"

He shook his head. "Don't what me."

God, since when did her lock stick? She tugged and jiggled, but the damn thing wouldn't turn. Meanwhile, Sarge's body heat was like an industrial-sized oven beside her. "I listened to your new album at work today."

A flicker of surprised pleasure crossed his face, but he hid it just as fast. "Yeah?"

"Mmm-hmm." She'd told River it was a podcast playing in her headphones, figuring she'd been honest with her friend enough for one day. "Were those...*thoughts* always bumping around in that head of yours? Or did they show up after you got stuck in a lightning storm or something?"

Sarge braced a hand on the doorframe and leaned closer. "Which thoughts are you referring to, Jas?"

"You know." Finally, she managed to get the door open—and not a moment too soon, since Sarge was licking his lips like a starved lion, ready to pounce. "The way you talk about women."

His boots *thunk*ed on the wood floor as he followed her into the apartment, shrugging off his coat as he entered. "Women *plural*, huh? Is that what you got from my songs?"

Jasmine hung her own coat in the hall closet, relieved to be facing away. "Oh, come on." *Don't. Don't doooo it.* "I'm sure there's been tons of opportunities on the road for…the kind of experience you need to write…those songs." *Callate estupida.*

Finished hanging her coat, Jasmine turned—and bit back a scream, nearly tumbling backward into the closet. Sarge was standing close—*so damn close*—with a displeased expression on his face. He looked older, wiser…and just a hint weary in a way that she tried not to let fascinate her. "I have to *feel* something to write a song. I have to *want*." He jabbed a hand through his hair, leaving it standing out at stray angles. "I've never felt *anything* close to that on the road. Ever. And I wouldn't call waking up to someone you don't recognize an opportunity. I wouldn't even give it a name because that might give it some importance."

A spiky ball rolled through Jasmine's chest. "Sarge, I didn't mean to—"

"It's fine." He closed his eyes a moment, opening to reveal just a flash of temper. Pain. "Just do me a favor? At least for tonight, try to pretend like you don't get a kick out of me with other people. Pretend it makes you fucking ill, the way I feel when I slip and imagine the reverse."

Jasmine was left standing on liquefied knees, heart knocking against her ribs as Sarge strode into her bedroom, the way a king might. She watched as he kicked off his boots, toeing them under her bed with a heated look over his shoulder. "You coming or do I need to come get you?"

"We haven't talked parameters yet." When his back stiffened, she felt a rush of frustration. "While you're here, while we…together this way, I don't want people in Hook to know about it."

He'd stopped moving. "You want to explain why?"

The frustration broke into winged pieces, demanding to be let free. "You haven't been here. You don't understand."

"Try me," Sarge said, facing her with a hooded expression.

"I…failed. Okay? I failed where you didn't. The most ambitious girl in town didn't even make it through the Lincoln Tunnel." She joined him in the room to begin digging through her underwear drawer, not looking for anything in particular, just needing an activity for her hands. "They've treated me differently since then. Carefully. With sympathy. If they know what we're doing, they'll see it for something it isn't. Me trying to recapture the success I never really had in the first place. Through you. You know they will."

Jasmine started when she felt Sarge's hands on her shoulders, his chest brush against her back. "I didn't realize they made you feel like that. I'm sorry." His lips traced up the back of her neck. "We know that's bullshit, Jasmine. That's what matters. If you need what we do to stay in this apartment, I won't fight you on it. But I will fight you on your theory that you failed."

When Sarge traced her earlobe with his tongue, she could only nod, even though the argument was one she'd already won in her head. "Not tonight, okay?"

Sarge turned her around, his eyes raking up and down her body. "Do you still have that blue dress, Jas?"

"Wait." She did a double take, certain she'd misheard him. "What now?"

He stepped away and took an unrushed turn around her room, pausing occasionally to stoop down and look at framed photographs. "The one you wore at the Feast of San Gennaro. When you sang that solo with the church choir. Do you remember?"

Did she remember? She thought about that day *constantly*. The feast was an Italian festival that took place once a year. Food vendors, contests, and various forms of entertainment took over the neighborhood for an entire week in September, although in recent years it had lost some of its traditional feel, becoming more modern and infused with pop culture to draw a younger crowd.

The year she enjoyed it the most, she'd been twenty-three, still trying to jump-start her flatlining music career. The choir director for Holy Cross Church, a lovely older woman named Adeline who liked to tip back an occasional whiskey sour during the day, had insisted Jasmine join the group for a solo on the main performance stage. When she wouldn't take no for an answer, Jasmine had relented. And *God*, it had been well worth giving up an hour with her date. That day marked the first and last time Jasmine performed for a riveted crowd, people gathering on sidewalks, climbing streetlamps to see her. She'd never sounded better in her life.

It was also the day she'd peaked.

"I don't remember seeing you there," Jasmine murmured.

Sarge picked up another photograph, this one of her and River. "I was across the street playing Whac-A-Mole. Or I was, anyway, until you started singing."

An uncomfortable lump formed in her throat. "Why would I still have that dress? It was worn out back then. It would be a total rag by now."

His glance in her direction was one of total confusion.

"Because you looked incredible in it." He set the picture down and turned. "Because when I picture you, it's in that blue dress."

"I don't *have* it," Jasmine insisted, far too quickly. There was a parting of gray skies taking place here, and she was terrified to know what they would reveal. *When I picture you.* How often did that happen? Since Sarge blew into town— had it only been two nights ago?—he'd been pursuing her. No hesitations. No momentary lack of focus on his goal...a goal that appeared to be *her.* The more he spoke and revealed, the more Jasmine wondered how far his crush extended. Did she *want* to know?

No. She didn't. Didn't want to be responsible for anything more than slaking the urges of her body. Eliminating the craving he'd originated in places she hadn't felt sparks as far back as she could remember. If she allowed that to happen while knowing there were deeper feelings involved on Sarge's part, the guilt and responsibility would keep her from experiencing the physical completion he was offering. The chance to have this captivating man close, so close, just for a while. Before he left and didn't come back, possibly for another four years.

Maybe for Sarge, this wasn't some long-carried torch. Maybe he just wanted to mark Jasmine off his spank bank list, the way men felt sentimental about their first taste of porn. The older woman he'd lusted after as a kid—no better time to satisfy that particular fantasy than on an impromptu visit home. While that possibility caused a suspicious ache deep in her stomach, it suited her far more than Sarge having feelings for her. Yes, it was much, *much* better. If he simply wanted his fantasy fulfilled, this was a two-way, solely physical street.

When Sarge had almost reached her, Jasmine took him off guard by meeting him halfway on that final step. The move brought their bodies flush, chest to knee, Sarge's erection pressing against her belly button. "I have the dress."

His upper lip twitched. "Put it on."

Jasmine smoothed her hands up his ridged chest, biting her lip over the dips and valleys. "Don't you want me naked?"

"*Yes*, I want you naked." He grazed a thumb down the side of her breast, sending a shudder of heat straight between her thighs. "I also want to be the one who made you naked. The *dress*, Jasmine."

It was hot. That was how Jasmine had to categorize a man remembering what you wore almost seven years earlier. Hot that he wanted that particular garment to be the thing he ripped off your body. Yes, hot. Not telling or emotional in any way.

Right.

With a slow brush of their bodies, she floated toward the closet, knowing she would find the blue dress at the back, hidden behind more recent purchases. She plucked it off the hanger and watched Sarge as she changed into it, buttoning the line of buttons that ran all the way down to the hem where it flirted midthigh. Sarge sat at the foot of bed, facing away. His pose was casual, but the line of tension in his shoulders looked as if it might snap him in two. They lifted and fell faster, faster…and some intuition told Jasmine she would find his eyes closed if she circled him. The vision made her heart pump faster.

"A few more parameters," she blurted, and watched Sarge's whip-tight muscles bunch even more through the cotton of his shirt. "If either one of us wants to bow out after tonight…no hard feelings."

His laughter was hollow. "Won't happen."

Jasmine smoothed her hands down the front of her dress, over the peaks of her breasts and lower to her stomach. "How do you know?"

Sarge whipped off his T-shirt and discarded it, giving her a view of his broad, sculpted back, the twin indentations at the base of his spine. *Those shoulders.* "There's a button I need to press on you," he rasped, his hands gripping his knees. "For the next few hours, finding that hot button and pressing it over and over is my life's fucking mission. If you want to bow out after that, it'll only be because I wore you out or rode you too hard. And you're too stubborn to admit either."

She sucked in an unsteady breath. "You probably shouldn't call a woman stubborn when you're trying to sleep with her."

"Stubborn is part of the reason I want her so bad. Any other rules?"

God, this man was dangerous to the detachment that was usually her salvation. He wouldn't stop saying things that made little lights go off in unused sections of her brain. "No."

"Good." She could tell by his flexing triceps that he'd begun unbuttoning his jeans. "Get over here, Jas, or I'm coming to get you."

Needing to give the flurries in her belly a moment to settle, Jasmine found her reflection in the mirror across the room. Most mornings, she couldn't even bear to look into her own exhausted eyes, but just then, she appeared the furthest thing from exhausted. In the blue dress she'd always associated with confidence, an exultant moment frozen in time, she looked… ripe for picking. Sexual. Even a little innocent, which made what was to come a hint more exciting. As if sex with a testosterone-charged, filthy-mouthed man needed the added stimulation.

Before she could lose the loose hold on her boosted self-image, Jasmine went to Sarge and rested her hands on his wide shoulders, purring when the muscles jumped beneath her palms.

His eyes blazed, mouth falling open with an agonized sound. Big hands snaked around the backs of her knees, yanking her into the vee of his thighs. Sarge's height put his mouth level with her pointed nipples, a position he took advantage of like a starving man, opening and closing his lips on her aroused, puckered flesh through the thin material of her dress. As he mouthed her breasts with low grunting noises, his touch slid higher, higher, to close around her bare bottom.

"Last time I saw you in this dress, I was sixteen." His fingers dug into her twin swells of flesh, tightening hard. "Everyone was looking at you. In awe of you. And I wanted to ask what took them so fucking long."

Without so much as a warning blink, Sarge twisted, using his grip on her backside to reverse their positions, landing her flat on her back on the bed. The hem of the dress fluttered up to rest at her waist, Jasmine's hands moving automatically to tug it down. But Sarge's hungry expression stopped her. His focus was nothing short of breathtaking. He'd apparently just glimpsed the promised land between her thighs, because he looked enraptured, tongue bathing his lips, big hands fisting the bedspread.

"Fuck, Jasmine. Look at your tight slit. Even after I had my fingers pumping inside you yesterday?" Shaking his head, he ran a thumb down her entrance, making her back arch on the bed. "I wondered if your pussy would be smooth as those thighs. Wondered if it would be parted a little so I could see your clit, but I can't see a goddamn thing. *God.*" He sucked his lower lip into his mouth, releasing it through his teeth. "You'd never know it from the way you ground on me earlier, but that blue dress was hiding something sweet, wasn't it?"

• • •

Refusing to take his gaze off her dampening center, Sarge ran his tongue along the inside of Jasmine's smooth thigh. Closer, closer, to the hottest sight he'd ever laid eyes on. Jasmine —

*his* Jasmine—with her legs parted, that blue dress rucked up around her hips. There was a bullish rise in his sternum, smoking out to fill his insides. He wanted to rear up with a shout, cover her with his body, and fuse their mouths together. Wanted to dry-fuck her with his aching dick until she was soaked and then fuck her like the world was ending. It was *painful* to hold back, but after last night, he was determined to give her more. Not some quick-on-the-trigger moron who didn't recognize the treasure laid out for his consumption. A treasure representing the curse he needed to break—and he couldn't do that if he lost himself.

Since he'd caught her off guard, she was still attempting to be modest, elegant fingers twisting in the hem, inching it down, which only made him twice as anxious to get his mouth on her flesh, to watch that caution shatter into a thousand pieces.

"Stop trying to be a good girl, baby." He parted her flesh with his middle finger, finding her wet enough to push inside with a satisfied noise. "We're here to be bad."

"Oh...*that's*. Am-mazing." Jasmine thighs writhed on either side of his wrist as he stroked in and out with his finger, breaking to tease her clit with the wetness. No, *no*...he wanted her legs spread. Wanted her with no other options or escape routes, save releasing against his lips and tongue and chin.

Sarge used his free hand to secure her right leg to the bed, shoving her other thigh open with his opposite elbow. "Watch my tongue." He waited until she followed his instructions before dragging his stiffened tongue through the center of her pussy, ending at her clit and pushing down hard. *Hard*. Until her hips were bucking, moans filling his ears. "You don't stay open so I can see every hot little inch of you, I won't do that again. Don't you want me to keep licking?"

"*Si*. Yes, *yes*."

"I know you do." Sarge trailed a series of kisses along her

delicate flesh. "You want it now. And you want to remember it later, too, so you can touch all the places I ate you. You want to remember the bad things I did."

The idea had come to Sarge out of nowhere—and it was entirely unlike him. But the uncontrollable impulse to immortalize the first time he brought her pleasure wouldn't leave him alone. He needed her to have proof, a memory of him as the man who'd been anything but plutonic while between her legs.

He gave her hip a gentle slap, continuing to tease her pussy with gentle bites and kisses. "Get your phone. I want you to play this back later when you're alone and my mouth and fingers aren't here to handle your ache."

Two frantic, sobbing breaths. "I can't do that."

"Yes, you can." He lapped once at her clit before lifting his head to lock gazes with passion-fogged brown eyes. "More than that, baby, you want to. You want to watch me do it all over later."

"I don't," she gasped.

"Liar." A quick scan of the room found her iPhone sitting on the bedside table. "Go on. You can reach it." Sarge turned his head to run his open lips up the inside of her left inner thigh. "I'll wait right here."

Jasmine threw her head back with a frustrated whimper, then made a grab for the phone, fingers fumbling to open the camera application. Sarge smiled against her skin as she lifted the device. And then it was on. The phone dropped to her belly the first time his tongue circled her clit, but he growled until she propped it back up. A pounding began in his head, inflicted by her taste, the way her flesh clenched when he slipped his tongue inside. *Tight little thing.* He couldn't get an adequate description in his head of what her taste reminded him of, so he lifted her ass in both hands, bringing her up to meet his mouth like a fucking meal.

Yeah, it turned him on knowing she'd be pressing play on these moments again later. He thought of her coming home from a long day of work and sagging back against the front door. Pulling out her phone and sliding her hand inside her jeans, legs slipping wide. He didn't expect the spark of jealousy to flicker in his chest. Maybe he didn't want her touching herself. It should be him.

It should always be him.

"Stop filming," Sarge ground out. "I'll do this for you any time you need it. You call me and I'll come. My tongue belongs right here."

"N-no. No." Her stomach shuddered down, forming a sexy hollow. "This was your idea. And I want it...want to remember...*oh*."

He attacked her with his mouth, out of heat, out of frustration he didn't quite know how to define. The possibility of living without this place between her thighs made him fucking crazed. Made him want to cause destruction. She liked having her clit sucked, so he executed the roll of his tongue, followed by prolonged suction until she finally dropped the phone with a muffled scream, fingers turning to fists in his hair.

"*Sarge. Ay que rico.* Don't stop. So close. *So close.*"

Hearing his name coated with lust straight from Jasmine's mouth sent a fresh bolt of need to his cock, thickening the neglected part where it snaked out from his unzipped fly. He needed to fist himself and pump until come shot from the tip, but she needed his fingers more, so he fucked himself against the bed's edge instead, groaning against her pussy as he thrust. Her thighs were starting to lift again, probably with the intention of locking around his head, but he wasn't having that. With rough hands, he shoved Jasmine's legs open and gave her one final chance to orgasm before he climbed up the bed and fucked her into delirium.

His middle finger and tongue wedged inside her entrance at the same time, rotating positions once, and that was all it took. Jasmine strained beneath him on the bed, hips lifting, thighs quaking, straight out of his dirtiest dreams. Her heels shoved against his shoulders, voice cracking, but he wouldn't stop. Wouldn't stop dragging his tongue over her clit, tasting what he'd done.

Only when her ankles finished their crusade to push him away did he allow himself to let up. Sarge prowled over her body, nudging her knees apart with his own. She still wore the blue dress, but it was beginning to wilt from the sweat he'd worked her into. Above the bodice, moisture dotted the swell of her bouncy tits. The ones he'd been thinking about since his body identified that his attraction and need belonged to one single person. One single woman.

"Gold. You taste like the color gold." Sarge dropped to his elbows, making a quick grab for the condom he'd placed within reach on the bedspread. No sooner had he covered his dick with latex than he pressed their bodies together, groaning as their lower bodies made first contact. "Warm. A little bit like cinnamon. Perfect." She whimpered as he jerked open a handful of the dress's buttons, exposing dusky-pink-tipped tits, pointing right at his mouth. "Made a fucking mess of this dress, didn't I?"

Sarge twisted his hips once and drove home, shouting a curse into the space above her head. *Oh God, I'm inside Jasmine and I'm so screwed she's perfect, perfect. Narrow and dripping and perfect.* She was climaxing around him already, struggling beneath him under the swiftness of her body's reaction, which didn't bode well for his plan to make this last. Making sure she found her peak was no longer a problem, so what was to prevent him from tossing her trembling legs over his shoulders and ending his own torment?

But she whimpered his name and everything inside him

seized. Jasmine. God, she was the most beautiful creature on the planet, and he wouldn't turn tonight into merely a fuck session.

"Baby." Sarge locked his arms beside her head, reared his hips back and rolled forward slowly, grinding down when he bottomed out. "Listened to my songs at work today, huh?"

"Yeah." Out of breath, she dug her nails into his ass and jerked him forward, into the squeeze of her body, even though he couldn't go any deeper. "Yeah, I listened."

He kissed her earlobe, used his lips to tug it, his tongue to play. "Did you make it to the last track?" He took her by surprise with a swift backward jerk of his hips and a teeth-chattering drive forward. "The one called 'Girl in Blue'?"

At that, Jasmine's eyes cleared a little, but Sarge didn't hold back. He'd bring her back to the brink, and he'd do it his way. But she wouldn't walk away from tonight with the notion she'd been laid. More needed to take place here. He couldn't hold back *everything* clawing at his insides, dying to break free.

"Did you wonder who that song was about?"

He hooked an arm beneath her knee and drew it up, up, until she moaned. "No...I-I didn't think—"

Sarge cut her off with a hot, openmouthed kiss. He didn't want to hear how oblivious she was to him. Didn't want to know the meaning of the song had been lost. Five seconds into their tongues sliding together in a seduction dance, and Jasmine's nails were biting into the flesh of his ass again, her hips tilting for another thrust of his cock. So he gave it to her good. He gave her another. And another, followed by the slap of his balls on her tight backside, until they were two desperate, groping pleasure slaves trying to rub the right spots that would just *please end the pain.*

"You feel that part of me smacking you? They've been full and hot all fucking day, needing to empty between these legs of yours. Does that make you hot, baby?" His pace was out of control, aggressive and unrelenting. "The way you lap-danced me like a stripper last night made me this way. I could barely think of you today without coming in my jeans again—and I thought of you *all day*."

*All my life.*

The pressure rising, rising in him was undeniable. His breath was coming in quick, dizzying pants, his precipice all the higher for knowing whose body would receive him. Jasmine. God, he'd never prepared for the possessiveness that hooked around his neck with a permanence that didn't scare him. Not at all. He'd known. Always know she was the ending for him.

Pouty lips parted, Jasmine's head tossed side to side on the bed. "Oh God, Sarge. This is bad. This is—" Her pussy clenched on a broken moan. "So *bad*."

Bad. What did she mean? He knew her body was satisfied, because he could still taste her pleasure. Could feel more on the way. Did she mean bad…because of who he was? Were they back to that? "What's bad, baby?" he murmured at her throat, taunting, licking the salt from her pulse. "Getting it from a younger man? One who was off-limits to you? *Bad girl*."

Her legs were wrapped around his hips like a python, hips lifting to meet his punishing rhythm, but her mouth whispered, "Stop…don't say those things."

"Do you mean that? Stop?" No answer, just an exposing of her throat, a biting of her lip, as she twisted beneath him. Jesus, he needed to release soon. Needed it more than food or oxygen. He was ramming his dick into Jasmine's slick entrance—slap, slap, slap—his body hovering over the promise of relief. It was right there. *Right there.* But the lines between him and Jasmine were so blurry and needed to be defined, or it would cheapen them. He didn't want her to see their being together as bad. Needed her to want him again when it was over.

Gritting his teeth on a tortured groan, Sarge fisted the base of his dick and drew it out of her heat. With the most substantial pain in his memory hanging between his thighs, he rolled Jasmine onto her stomach, slid his cock up the crevice of her bottom, then pushed home inside her pussy once again, shaking with the power of being back where he belonged.

"Is this what you need, Jasmine?" Sarge pumped, his sweaty body meeting the underside of her curved ass. Licking perspiration from his lips, he shook out his right hand and accompanied his drives with a slap of her backside. A second and third. "You don't hand out the punishments anymore, babysitter, in your short, teasing skirts. It's my turn now." *So close. It hurt. So close.* No more waiting, the come was shooting up his cock, gripping his body with near-paralyzing bliss. Sarge fell flush with her body, his hips pistoning out of control, *fucking, fucking, fucking.* About to explode, he dropped his mouth into her hair. "I might be younger, but I'm not *young.* I'm a man and I'm fucking you blind. I'm *your* man. Say it."

"*You're my man,*" Jasmine sobbed, her inner walls gripping him as he shot off all his pent-up need into the sweetest spot on earth, reveling in her climaxing for a third time. It went on forever, her milking body leaching him of seed, his hoarse shouts ricocheting off the walls and ceiling. His hands were all over her, stroking her hair, her shoulders, her ass, as the pleasure spiraled through him, rearranging everything in its path. Changing him for good.

Finally spent, he slipped free of her body and fell to the bed, pulling her backward into an unbreakable hold before his worst fear happened and she tried to get away, close herself in the bathroom or somewhere he couldn't see or touch or talk to her. He wouldn't deal well with that. *At all.* Not after what they'd done. Not after she'd engraved her name on his soul.

He thought the inscription had already been there, but it was so much more prominent now.

Get her out of his system? Break the curse?

He'd been a blind idiot thinking he could accomplish such a thing. Or to think he'd even *want* to rid himself of Jasmine's claim on his being. No. Never. Right now, lying there exposed, the very idea scared him.

"Sarge," Jasmine said, still sounding out of breath. "I—"

"Shh. I know. You're going to tell me I'm not your man. Not permanently." Striving for casual even though his gut was sinking under the weight of her cautious tone, he traced his fingers over her naked hip, up the inside of her arm. "I am *tonight*, though. I'm your man until further notice. And your man should hold you like you might escape. Because you not being here when he woke up maybe sounds like the worst thing in the world. Okay?"

There was a long pause wherein Sarge could practically hear her pulse skittering and racing and dipping. "Okay."

His eyelids slid shut, tension fading from his neck. "Thank you."

He tucked Jasmine's head beneath his chin and dropped off, dreaming of the color gold.

# Chapter Nine

Jasmine shoved a hank of hair out of her face and stumbled into the kitchen.

Jesus H. Christ.

She tightened her short terry cloth robe around her body even though you could probably fry an egg on her backside. Sunlight filled her tiny kitchen, and she squinted into the light, waiting for her eyes to adjust. Behind her in the bedroom, she could hear Sarge's sturdy frame moving on her creaky bed, probably taking a much-needed breather after...*after.*

It was safe to say she'd learned one valuable lesson this morning. There were worse ways to wake up than with a gorgeous, naked man whispering a husky prayer against your lady parts. Giving thanks to the Lord above in between drags of his tongue through your hypersensitive flesh.

*Dear God, thank you for making this so sweet for me. Thank you for this woman who opens her thighs for my hungry mouth. Thank you...thank you...*

Jasmine laid a hand on her forehead. Yeah, there were worse things. After the second time he'd brought her to a bone-melting orgasm with his mouth, she'd begged him to stop the torment, but he'd kept going. And going. True to his word the night before, he hadn't allowed her to leave bed until her body was covered in sweat, stubbornly refusing to push his ready erection inside her.

She had a good idea what his refusal to finish was about, too. Knew he would torment her all day with the knowledge that he was in need. In need of *her*. Even now, she could barely stand knowing. This temporary tryst felt the furthest thing from casual, especially after Sarge's revelation over the song. He'd written a *song* about her, about something she'd worn one day six years ago. Somewhere in the dark last night, with Sarge's chest lifting and falling at her back, she'd allowed herself to consider the possibility that Sarge's feelings ran deeper than she'd originally thought.

If that was the case, she shouldn't allow this affair to go on. Sarge might have grown up—*understatement*—but he was still River's brother. Continuing to sleep with him when buds of feelings were starting to spring up everywhere, leaves pushing open, bright flowers blooming…it was a terrible idea. With a lucrative contract just waiting for his signature, what did she expect him to do? Stay in Hook? In just a few days, she would be a thirty-year-old woman. A woman who'd adjusted her life's ambitions from singer/songwriter to factory floor manager. She had no business trying to tie down this talented, charismatic—not to mention *famous*—man who was nursing the residual glow of his first crush.

It needed to stop. Distancing herself as of this morning was the wisest course of action, even though Sarge would push back. She knew he would, no question. Having that much certainty about a man's character was terrifying in itself. Even more terrifying, however, was the certainty that same man would look at her one day and wonder why he'd settled for a Jersey girl who wore a jumpsuit and goggles to work.

Feeling pressure behind her eyes, Jasmine picked up the frying pan sitting on her stove and slammed it back down. She used to overflow with confidence. Used to laugh when anyone had the *cojones* to doubt her. How had she landed here?

Footsteps moved behind her in the form of groaning floorboards, but Jasmine didn't turn around, choosing instead to yank open cabinets in search of a granola bar to throw in her purse for lunch. But when the plucked strains of guitar strings filled the kitchen, she froze, still on her tiptoes.

"Morning," Sarge said. "Everything okay in here?"

She started rooting around again, shoving aside boxes of rice and a bag of flour. "I have breakfast with my father on Friday mornings. He'll be here any second to pick me up."

A masculine grunt of acknowledgment. It didn't sound pleased. Well, too bad. It was the truth. Her Friday breakfasts with Paulie were tradition and she wouldn't break it. Their breakfasts—and Jasmine's sporadic visits to her parents' house in Hook—were a comfort to her. Falling back into the familiar rhythm of speaking Spanish, listening to her father use phrases not spoken in New Jersey, reminded her of where she'd come from and the people who loved her. She wouldn't cancel just so she could try her hand at seducing Sarge back into bed. Giving him the same treatment he'd woken her with. Jasmine's face heated. Those thoughts were in direct violation of her resolve. Dangerous.

"Help yourself to whatever you want. There are eggs…" Jasmine turned to find Sarge, naked save a low-slung pair of boxer briefs, guitar draped around his shoulders. The combination of his finger-abused hair—courtesy of her—and that narrowed-eyed, considering look made her skin tingle.

"What are you doing tonight?"

Jasmine scrambled for an excuse to stay away from the apartment, away from him, before realizing she didn't have to fabricate a single thing. "There is a retirement party tonight for one of the machine mechanics. That's what I'm doing."

He plucked an easy combination of strings that had the nerve to sound incredible. "Let me guess. This party is at the Third Shift?"

A reluctant smile tugged her lips. "Is there anywhere else in this town?"

His jaw went tight. "Is that prick going to be there?"

It took Jasmine a few beats to recall exactly *which* prick Sarge referred to. After all, she worked with quite a few of them. "Oh, Carmine?" She feigned nonchalance, playing with the tie of her robe. "Yes, he probably will."

A darker, more complicated scale of chords, played without taking his gaze off her. "Are you going to invite me or do I just show up?"

Jasmine crossed her arms. "Oh, are those my two options?"

"Yeah." He took a step toward her. "So pick one."

Outrage stiffened her spine and released a fog of heat into her throat. It felt...*phenomenal*. She hadn't been good and mad in a long time. There hadn't been anything worth invoking her wrath. Now, though, she let the irritation trickle down into her fingertips, which curled themselves into fists. When satisfaction crossed Sarge's handsome, stubbled face, Jasmine realized his aim had been to anger her. Why? "Is there a reason you're pissing me off in my own kitchen?"

"Yeah." He jerked the guitar over his head—sending his muscles dancing in mesmerizing patterns—and set the instrument down with a *thunk*. "I didn't like the way you looked when I walked in here."

Something heavy flipped over in her stomach. "It's seven thirty in the morning. Were you expecting a flamenco dance?"

His full male laughter put a dent in her anger. "I wouldn't turn one down." He prowled toward the fridge and opened it, giving her an eyeful of his profile, complete with the fat, unsatisfied bulge in his underwear. Which she would clearly be thinking about for the rest of the day. "So, Paulie's got breakfast covered. Can you wait while I make you lunch?"

Jasmine crossed her arms to hide her distended nipples. Since when did triple orgasm recipients get hot and bothered again after mere minutes? "You can't just piss me off and then make me lunch."

Smile playing on his lips, Sarge lifted his head, sending dark hair falling over his eye. "Why is that?"

"A sandwich is an easy way off the hook." She pursed her lips. "Too easy."

*Good God*, she was flirting with him. How had he managed to flip her mood around when she'd been mired in dread upon entering the kitchen? She was shameless and utterly self-destructive. None of that seemed to matter, however, when Sarge closed the refrigerator door and sauntered toward her. "If you don't wait while I make you lunch…" He propped his hands on the counter, blocking her in. "I guess I'll just have to bring it down to the factory later."

"You can't just walk in there. You'll be mobbed," Jasmine breathed. "Besides, we have a cafeteria."

He came closer, crowding, giving her a mouthwatering whiff of man. "It's not good enough for you." His fingers teased the hem of her robe, forming goose bumps down her legs. "Go get dressed while I make you something."

"Stop being so pushy."

"Stop being so beautiful."

There was no way around his magnetism. Not when they were both half dressed, the morning after sex so good she'd thought it impossible. Not when sincerity threaded his deep voice. Not when he was looking down at her like she might be the only other living, breathing person in the world. And maybe they needed to keep having the impossible sex because it was the only way to continue the human race. Really, it would just be for science. They'd be humanitarians.

*I'm losing my damn mind.* She lost it even more when he tilted his head and rubbed that bulge against the knot of her robe, side to side, in slow, devastating drags. "Let me feed you."

"No." Jasmine tried to back up, but there was nowhere to go, pinned between his big body and the counter, watching his abs flex as he rubbed against her. "The scales are too imbalanced here."

"Why?" His expression mirrored the confusion in his voice. "Because of what we did in bed this morning?"

"What *you* did, Sarge," she whispered, shocked to feel a flush climb her neck. Men did not turn her red. Ever. They didn't immobilize her under a single look, either. Didn't drape her insides in warm, sticky silk.

Jasmine's thoughts were cut off when Sarge framed her jaw in one big hand, tilting her head back. "Baby." He applied gentle pressure to her cheeks, forcing her mouth to open on a gust of breath. "Eating your pussy isn't a chore, it's a privilege."

"Stop," she tried to say, but it emerged as a moan. A moan that turned to a whimper when the hand not holding her jaw slipped between their bodies. Down, down, deft fingers making quick work of her robe tie and pushing it open. Sarge's grip found the apex of her thighs, cupping her through cotton panties.

"You want *more*, Jasmine." It wasn't a question. "Feel my dick? It got the best last night and doesn't want anything else. It *needs* more. Needs to feel you again so bad. Especially now that we know your pussy is a size too small for me."

"*Sarge*," she gasped, moving on his hand, going up on her tiptoes seeking a firmer hold, which he gave her in spades, molding, squeezing. Owning.

"I know," he grated, the words vibrating where he laid them on her mouth. "I know, baby. Come back to me tonight and get what's coming to you."

Jasmine's frustrated cry filled the kitchen. "You're playing dirty."

His tongue licked up her jawline and slid into her mouth, nudging hers in an invitation to come play. Jasmine's eager participation was short, though, when he broke the kiss before she was even close to satisfied. Catching her off guard, Sarge lifted her legs up around his waist and dry-fucked her against the counter. Buried his face in her neck and pumped, three, four, five times, before dropping her back down. "You haven't seen dirty yet, Jas," he rasped into her ear. "I saw your face when I walked in, and you're not getting rid of me that easily. Now go get dressed while I make you lunch. I hear your father honking outside."

After he had to physically prop her up against the counter, his arrogant walk back to the fridge should have made her indignant. It should have had her throwing a blunt object at the back of his head. Instead it had her admitting quietly that even with her newfound appreciation for Sarge, she'd severely underestimated him.

She just managed to keep her feminine pride intact five minutes later when she dodged his attempt to kiss her while walking out the door. Carrying the sack lunch he'd handed her.

His laughter echoed in Jasmine's ears the entire car ride to breakfast.

• • •

The problem with trying to keep a woman coming back for more was…the waiting. It had been years since Sarge had this kind of free time on his hands, usually packing up and moving to a new city after only one gig. His days on tour were filled with phone calls with the press, annoying photo shoots, morning interviews at local radio stations, sound checks, and playing mediator to James and Lita. There wasn't a lot of time left over for thinking. And he had a shitload to think about.

Jasmine had walked out of her apartment only thirty

minutes ago, although it felt like a week. Now that he'd acknowledged that his bonehead game plan of fucking Jasmine out of his mind once and for all was nothing more than a pipe dream, he needed a new course of action. And if he blocked out all the noise in his head and focused on what felt like necessity, Sarge couldn't think past holding on to Jasmine as long as she'd allow it. Going back on the road had seemed like a given when he arrived in Hook. It *wasn't* a given now. Simple as that. There was more than lust between him and Jasmine, but if he needed to use their attraction as a means to spend more time with her—until she saw he was for real—so be it. No one would catch him complaining.

Mentally replaying the phone calls he'd just made, he could admit without ego that he had a few tricks up his sleeve.

Truth was, the last year on the road had been shitty. He'd stopped chasing a way over Jasmine by sleeping around after two years away from Hook, but nothing he did regained what he'd lost by repeatedly giving up that part of himself. That part of himself he'd always felt he should be hanging on to. Fine, what he'd learned about women over those two blurry years was clearly being appreciated by Jasmine now, but just knowing he'd honed those intuitions with others made him nauseous. It had never felt good. Not the way it did last night. He was ruined for anyone else. Maybe he had been since the first time Jasmine walked into his living room.

There was a battle ahead, and not just to keep Jasmine in his life. Something had turned down the volume on the music inside her. She still painted the air with life everywhere she went, but it was subdued, and it shouldn't be. Not from someone so amazing. But Sarge understood the feeling all too well. After the lights went off and the screaming crowd went home, he'd just been left with himself and his choices. That wasn't an easy thing when somehow your choices had made you instead.

One such regret was his stupid belief that a monthly

check was all his sister needed from him the last four years. Which is what brought him to Holy Cross Church's doorstep, blowing warm breath into his cupped palms while waiting for Adeline, the choir director, to arrive. Anyone in Hook knew, if you wanted gossip without asking for it, you paid a visit to Adeline. She had a habit of talking to herself within earshot of anyone who would listen in—although Sarge always suspected she stirred the pot on purpose. Knowing River, though, she wouldn't tell him without a fight how the last four years had been. And he needed to know so he could help.

"Never say that's Sarge Purcell waiting on me." He turned just in time to see Adeline slap her knee, lipstick-smeared teeth spreading into a genuine smile he couldn't help but return. "I heard you were back in town and I said, send that boy to see me. Who was it that sent you? Was it Gerald at the tobacco shop?" Adeline trudged past him, fumbling with her keys. "Nasty gambling habit, that one," she muttered on the way.

Same old Adeline. Funny how when he'd left Hook, he'd been disgusted by its inability to change. Now, though, he was glad as hell it remained the place stored in his memory. "How's the choir shaping up for next year?" Sarge asked, following Adeline into the church office.

"Oh, fair enough, I suppose. A few squeaky wheels, a blown tire or two." She said something under her breath that sounded like *goddamn Debbie*. "What do they want from us, though?" Her eyebrows bobbed underneath her eyeglass frames. "We're not big fancy professionals like you."

"We're not fancy, but we get by," Sarge murmured, dropping into the chair she indicated. "River asked me to play a song or two on Christmas Eve."

That was the only prompt the choir director needed. "That sister of yours, Sarge. I tell you, there isn't a single bad word a body could say against her. And after everything she's been through."

"Right." A lump formed in Sarge's throat. When River and her high school sweetheart broke up, Sarge had just left Hook, caught up in the whirlwind that came with earning a contract and being thrown into a recording studio with three seemingly incompatible strangers. "All she's been through."

"I thought that man would come to his senses when she got pregnant with Marcy, but I was wrong. Haven't seen hide nor hair of him since he rolled back into Hook after being discharged. Only stayed in town long enough to break your sister's heart, then off he went, the bastard."

*Ah, Jesus.* River had led him to believe the breakup with Vaughn had been a mutual decision. But it hadn't. She'd been pregnant and abandoned. Had she even been truthful with their parents about the situation? Strange enough, he remembered Vaughn as a stand-up guy, if clearly troubled. One who'd been crazy about River since Sarge could remember. Obviously he'd been way off about the man who'd dated his sister through high school. "Vaughn's uncle still in town, or…?" Sarge managed around the razor blades he'd swallowed.

"No, he made for Florida when Vaughn enlisted. Do you know he never once set foot into the Sunday church service? Not when he was raising Vaughn and not after," Adeline said, lowering her glasses as if she'd just imparted the worst transgression known to man. "I think his apartment above the stationery store is still empty, which should tell you something about the real estate market in Hook. Dead as a doornail."

"Sign's still broken over the stationery shop?"

"That's the way things stay when you're cheap as dirt." Adeline patted her hair. "Ask your sister about cheap. That man she's working for would risk his life to save a penny from being run over."

Sarge couldn't help but chuckle at that. "The factory owner?"

"Nope!" Adeline slapped both hands onto the desk.

"That run-down house of sin she's working in three nights a week. Cocktail waitressing, if that's what you call donning a skirt and parading around with a tray." For some reason she put the word "tray" in quotation marks, but Sarge was too stunned to explore why.

He leaned forward slowly in his chair. "We're still talking about River?"

"Yes, sir." The old woman huffed. "You can't blame me for passing on news. I just assumed you knew."

With a jolt, Sarge realized he'd come to his feet. "No...of course. I don't blame you. I'm glad I know." He remembered the shock of seeing his notoriously peppy sister looking so exhausted, framed by the doorway of their childhood house. Hadn't he decided then and there to help River? To make up for his four-year absence by doing a hell of a lot more than sending checks? Better get started. "You wouldn't happen to have a phone number for Vaughn, would you, Adeline?"

"No, I do not." Adeline lit a cigarette and blew a stream of smoke at the ceiling. "But I have an address for him."

"How?"

Adeline took another long drag of nicotine, watching him over her fingers. "When Vaughn's uncle left town, he left behind some furniture and the landlord said the church could have a look, see what was worth keeping. I found a few envelopes from Vaughn among his things. Nothing inside, but there was a return address." Cigarette in her mouth, Adeline rooted through the top drawer of her desk before pulling out a sealed envelope and handing it to Sarge. "Don't make me regret I gave that to you."

"I won't." Sarge turned from the desk, dropping a heavy hand on the doorknob. "I'm going to take care of it."

She clicked her desk drawer shut and inclined her head. "See that you do."

# Chapter Ten

They never broke routine at the factory. If the cogs didn't turn, the product didn't ship on time. If the products didn't ship on time, money didn't exchange hands. Which meant the floor workers didn't get paid. Like Jasmine, most of her coworkers lived paycheck to paycheck, and having their salary docked spelled disaster. So when the bell rang for quitting time at three o'clock, instead of five, everyone on the floor kept working, assuming it had been in error.

Until it rang again.

Beside Jasmine, River tossed down her clipboard and pushed the goggles up onto her head. "Maybe it's a fire drill?"

Jasmine hummed in her throat. "I'm not stopping until I smell smoke."

The bell rang a third time, making both women frown. Jasmine stopped in the process of applying her machine to the waiting metal plate when the head boss's droning voice thrummed over the loudspeaker. "Factory is closing early today. Clear your station and head out." A loud sigh was accompanied by static. "There's pizza and beer in the parking lot. This is a one-shot deal, so don't get used to it."

A cheer went up at the same moment the machines ceased their clanging, making the elated laughs and whistles extra loud. Seeing River light up with a smile of disbelief told Jasmine to stow her skepticism. There *had* to be a catch. She'd been working in the factory long enough to know their boss wasn't a generous man. But she wasn't going to ruin her best friend's—or anyone else's—fun.

Around them, factory employees cleaned up their stations in a hurry, dashing toward the locker rooms to change back into street clothes and warm coats. Jasmine and River were caught up in the flow of chaos, losing track of each other until twenty minutes later when they filed down the hallway into the back parking lot. When the double doors swung open, Jasmine's mouth fell open. Coolers of beer sat in the backs of pickup trucks, pizza boxes being passed among the crowd of bewildered factory workers. It took her a few seconds to decipher the source of her sudden suspicion, but the music pumping from one of the trucks' speakers finally penetrated her shock.

Old News played, but it wasn't just any song. "Girl in Blue," in its dirty, bass-heavy glory, filled the parking lot. Just like that, she knew Sarge was behind their early dismissal. The realization spread a foreign sensation through her body, kind of like that weird stage after you'd been hit in the funny bone. When you can't decide if the feeling is pain or pleasure.

River distracted Jasmine by grabbing her arm. "I'm going to grab some pizza. You coming?"

Jasmine tried not to be obvious about scanning the crowded parking lot for Sarge. "Go ahead. I'll catch up in a minute."

"'Kay," River trilled, bouncing off toward the circle of trucks.

One of her coworkers pressed a cold Bud Light into

Jasmine's hand. She took it and leaned against the factory wall, an amused smile playing around her lips to see her coworkers so animated. Someone had already produced a football, which was being tossed dangerously close to the crowd, but no one seemed to care. Warm breath puffed into the December air, reddening faces and forcing people to huddle together. It wasn't perfect by most definitions, but to them, it was paradise.

A dense gray cloud passed over the winter sun, casting a shadow over the parking lot. Almost on cue, the song restarted, seemingly louder, stopping Jasmine's breath from leaving her throat. "Girl in Blue" was like being trapped inside a human chest. The thick, sexy drumbeat that couldn't find an exact rhythm, picking up and dropping out without warning. *Boom. Boomboomboom. Boom.* Like an erratic heartbeat. The bass line was low and heavy, transmitting the sense of an impending storm. A warning. Vibrating guitar chords joined the fray off and on, unable to make up their mind. And all that happened before Sarge's voice sneaked up and pounced.

> *I need tending. Never ending.*
> *Want that, need that, girl in blue.*
> *No panty lines, no ties, no binds.*
> *Got me hard up over you.*

As the song played, Jasmine could hear her own breath scraping up her chest, drifting out over her lips in a white puff. Could feel her toes curling in her shoes. Was everyone looking at her? No. No, they weren't. She was the only one who knew Sarge had written the song about her. Jasmine took a long pull of beer, but the alcohol only turned up the heat inside her, the slow slide of it down her middle feeling like a caress. She closed her eyes, images flickering against the backdrop of her eyelids like an X-rated movie. Sarge releasing his length from his pants, the way it dropped and bobbed in the space between her legs.

> *Grip those hips,*
> *Up into you*
> *Raging, pushing, letting go*
> *Biting mouths, suck those roses*
> *Once not enough*
> *Flipped over. Round two.*

Wetness rushed to the spot that had been so well loved by Sarge's mouth that morning. *Just that morning.* How could she be this needy? It took a concerted effort to keep her breath from rasping like she'd run a marathon. Her palms were slicking up and down her squeezing thighs, creating friction through her leggings. Hot. So hot. So hot.

When the cell phone buzzed in her front right pocket, a gasp tripped over her lips, the vibration almost enough to send her flying. She knew who called before even answering. "Hello?"

"Jasmine." Sarge's gruff voice transported her back to the darkness of her bedroom, taking her miles away from the bustling parking lot.

"Where are you?" she whispered, even though she could hear "Girl in Blue" playing down the line, meaning he was close to the parking lot. Watching her?

"I'm close." How did he make those two words sound so filthy? "Pull up the video on your phone. The one we made last night. I want to see you watch it."

Excitement almost buckled Jasmine's knees, even as she spoke her denial. "I'm not watching that here. I can't."

"Why not?" His voice was deep, abrasive. "Your pussy can't get any wetter than it already is, Jasmine. I *see* you."

Jasmine sucked in a breath, pressing end on the call in

an attempt to rein in the compulsion to follow Sarge's orders. She couldn't—*wouldn't*—do something so inappropriate with her coworkers and best friend surrounding her. But she wanted to. The damn song must have been on repeat, because the intro started again, calling to the pit of her belly, twisting it in a knot. All day, she'd resisted watching the video, but right now…right now, it felt impossible. Beneath her winter coat, her nipples strained, the damp seam of her leggings rubbed against the ache. Watching the video wouldn't help her situation, but Sarge would. Had it gone unsaid that he would come to her once she followed his directions? Or was that wishful thinking?

With a muttered curse, Jasmine swiped the screen of her phone and pulled up the video application, hitting play on the last recorded option before her nerve deserted her.

Jasmine almost dropped the device as a loud moan emerged from the speaker, but she quickly lowered the volume, relieved when no one seemed to notice. And then there was only Sarge, tongue flicking against her most private flesh, his big hands holding her thighs open as he watched her. His blue eyes were glazed as if he'd just smoked opium, mouth working, working. From the angle she'd held the phone, the erection hanging between his legs was visible…and that was what drew her attention, even more than his masterful mouth. She wasn't in the mood for foreplay. *No.* Being filled was all that mattered.

It was only when Sarge's name appeared on her vibrating phone and she answered that Jasmine realized her whole body was shaking. "Where?" she breathed.

Sarge sounded like a dying man when he responded. "Side entrance, baby. Hurry."

Jasmine took a moment to make sure no one was watching before speed-walking along the factory's perimeter and slipping around the corner. Sarge paced in the alleyway, his hair a total mess. When he saw her, the growl that emerged from his mouth made her loins tighten like belt. They met in a tangle of limbs, mouths devouring in wet slides of tongue and bumping teeth, Sarge's hands unzipping her jacket to get their bodies flush. Reason deserted Jasmine. She didn't *care* how Sarge got their lower bodies locked together, so long as it was now. Now. As their mouths mated in a frantic dance, she could see the video from her phone. His worshipping mouth, his forceful hands, the way he'd reached down to wrap a fist around his arousal every time she moaned his name.

Sarge broke the kiss. "Inside. Have to get inside." He cupped her breasts, lifted and kneaded. "Much as I'd like everyone to know I'm the one making you this goddamn hot, I'd have to beat them off you with a stick afterward." Dipping his head, he nipped at the tips of her breasts in turn. "And I want this all to myself. I want to guard you and feed you and fuck you."

Did that send another shot of liquid slicking down to her core? God, yes. She was dying a slow death, the longer it took to get Sarge inside her. But nothing could stop those insecurities from rearing their ugly heads. They were always present, just waiting for an opening to sing their solo. "You want this so bad?" Her laughter was half breathless, half skeptical, maybe a little sad. "You can still see the outline of my goggles."

His disbelief was capped with annoyance when he pulled away, wedging her face between his hands. "You listen to me, I've been to twenty-nine countries and stared out at millions of faces, and…" He ran frustrated blue eyes over her face. "No one's lip turns up the way yours does. No one's chin is as stubborn as yours while still being so stupid cute. No one looks like they can keep all my secrets. Or be the reason for all my secrets. They only built *one* of you. So no more. I'm shutting that shit down right now."

Sarge gripped her shoulders and backed her toward the side entrance, reaching around her hip to pry the door open. They were ensconced in darkness, his intensity boring down on her, shredding her up inside as the door slammed. An overhead grate allowed thin slits of sunlight into the silent machine room, giving her shifting views of harsh planes of his face, the heat in his eyes, as her back met a concrete wall. "Sarge—"

He cut her off with his seeking mouth, kissing her until air became necessary to staying conscious, determined hands working the fly of her jeans. "*You.*" His forehead bumped into hers. "You don't make jokes about how bad I need you. Feeling like I might die without you wrapped around me isn't funny."

"I'm sorry," Jasmine breathed, meaning it. How could she *not* mean it when his voice shook, when his words were slamming into her chest like unruly bumper cars? The situation was getting away from her, the morning's resolve nothing but a distant echo. There wasn't a precipice in sight she could hold on to to pull her out of the quicksand. "I didn't mean to make fun. It's just…the way you're making me behave." Something about the near-darkness sent honesty tumbling out. "I've never had trouble putting the brakes on before. The first time shouldn't happen when I'm thirty, right? I shouldn't…I shouldn't…"

"*What?*" The word emerged like an expletive against her ear. "You shouldn't want a man who walked around all morning feeling sick? For passing up a chance to bang your sweetness up against the kitchen counter?" He dragged the jacket off her shoulders, letting it drop to the floor with a *whoosh*, before planting his hands over her head. "I'm sick as fuck, Jasmine. Cure me."

*This is what it feels like to be craved.* Beyond reason. Beyond anything in her experience. His pain called to an untapped facet of her womanhood and dug in, knitting loose ends together. There was a thrill that came with knowing you'd caused a man's desperation and you were the only one who could fix it. The only one capable of negating his aches by driving them higher, higher, before letting him down. Sarge had started a boil this morning by denying her the chance to reciprocate the pleasure he'd given. Now the boil rollicked and bubbled over her edges, sizzling down her sides, rousing the dormant seductress housed inside her.

Jasmine hooked a finger in Sarge's belt loop and tugged his hips forward, smiling when his breath rushed out in the form of her name. *Jasmine.* "When I was watching the video?"

"Yeah?" he prompted.

She cupped his erection through his jeans, pulse picking up speed at her own bravery, at the weight of him. "I couldn't look away from this."

Sarge groaned, tilting his hips to push himself into her palm. "Did you see me fucking your bed I needed inside your pussy so bad?"

"Yes," she whispered, giving him a firmer grip. "But that's not what you want right now, is it?"

"*I always want it,*" he growled, ramming his fist into the cement wall. "I want to be pumping inside you every minute of the day."

*Good Lord.* It took Jasmine a moment to come down from the potency of his statement. There were two sides of her battling for supremacy inside Jasmine. The terrified side, worrying Sarge wanted more than she could give—and the side dying to give him everything. In the darkness, with their bodies primed for only one thing, logic was the weaker opponent. Her thighs rubbed together, her teeth raking over her lips like an all-out addict whose drug of choice was *this man. Only* this man. *Now.*

Jasmine unbuttoned Sarge's jeans and slowly lowered the

zipper, noticing that he held his breath. "Do you ever think of me on my knees?"

His laugh turned to a gritted curse when she fondled his hardness, pulling it from his jeans and running light fingertips over every ridge and vein. "Ah, Jesus. You don't want to know how often I think of that, baby." His forehead dropped down onto her shoulder. "You've sucked my cock in every hotel shower across Europe."

The apex of her thighs contracted—a swift tug of muscles. "But it was all in your head." Using one hand to grip his length, she found his balls and massaged, her eyelids falling when his body jerked on a moan. "I want to give you the real thing."

Back and forth, his head shook on her shoulder. "I'll come too fast. You need me between your legs. The song… the video. I know you need fucking."

Despite his denial, she could hear the lust coating his voice. He wanted inside her mouth. She was aching to give herself to him that way. There was no stopping this. Jasmine went down on her knees between his body and the wall, pushing away his halfhearted attempts to keep her standing. "You'll give that to me later, won't you?"

His eyes blazed, hands clenching in her hair. "Jesus, don't tell me from your knees that you want me to fuck you later, Jas. I won't last a minute."

Had she ever felt this alive? This daring? She swirled her tongue around the slick, engorged tip. "But I do want that. So bad."

Sarge's groan rang in her ears. "Fuck this. Stand up so I can rip the panties I made wet right off your sex-kitten ass."

Jasmine's response was to glide her mouth halfway down his shaft, maintaining eye contact as she sucked her way back to the tip. Sarge fell forward, his lips parting on a silent shout of pleasure. His palms slapped onto the wall behind her, leaving him bent at the waist, legs spread shoulder width apart. As if the move were unconscious, but he wanted to get all of himself as close as possible, Sarge gathered his shirt in a fist and lifted, giving her a front-row seat to his flexing stomach.

"Baby, baby, that's so good. Feels so good riding on your tongue. My stomach hurts already just knowing…knowing it's you. Won't last, goddammit…I can't."

His face was a mask of pleasure, eyes struggling to stay open but squeezing shut every few seconds when she sucked a little more of him. The taste of salt was already spreading on her tongue, evidence of his lust that couldn't be contained. She lifted his heavy arousal toward his belly to lick the underside, turned on to see how tightly his balls were drawn up. Close, he was already *so close*, and having witnessed his unbelievable stamina last night, the obvious desire wrought by her mouth was a huge turn-on. Her heart was beating triple time in her chest, wetness rushing between her legs. Without conscious thought, she palmed the twin globes of hanging flesh and gloried in the sound of him releasing a string of curses.

"That's it. That's it. Feel me getting ready?" His thighs started to shake on either side of her face. "You…*no*. Jasmine, baby. You stop now. I'm…oh my God I'm going to lose it so hard. I'm thinking of fucking you. Fucking you. Fucking you. Get up. I can't stop it."

Greedy. She was greedy for Sarge. His shaft was so full inside her mouth, so stiff. His hands were punishing fists in her hair, made all the hotter because he likely wasn't even aware how much they pulled. He was just a hungry male trying to get his mate's mouth closer, tighter. When she felt his fullness jerk, heard Sarge's voice choke off into rough pants, she reached around his hips to dig her fingernails into his ass, hard enough to leave marks, tugging him closer as he spent himself down her throat.

"*Fuuuuuck*." His hips gave two uneven rolls. "It can't…be this…good. *Jesus*."

Jasmine lost her balance, partially because of Sarge moving against her mouth, but mostly because of the incessant rounds of heat blasting her. One after another, until she tipped to the side, felled by the power of his climax. She'd done that? Yeah…she'd *done* that.

"*Up*," Sarge growled, gripping Jasmine's elbows and hauling her into a standing position. And *ohhh*, what a knockout punch to have his giant, satisfied body towering above her, still semierect and dripping onto the ground. Her fingers twitched, desperate to dip inside her jeans and give pressure to her swollen clit. Time wasn't allotted to her, however, because Sarge had other plans.

He turned Jasmine toward the wall and pressed forward, forcing her hands up to stabilize her. A breathless moment passed wherein she could feel him forming intentions with a sweep of his gaze. Jasmine found herself arching her back, offering her bottom up for his perusal. "Did you like that, *mi rey*?"

"What did you call me?" Sarge's chest was flush with her back in a split second, his mouth messing up her hair, fingers fumbling with the zipper of her jeans. "Call me that again while my fingers are in your pussy."

Fragments of light shot through Jasmine's vision when Sarge's touch delved into her panties and thrust home with two fingers. "*Mi rey*. Don't stop, my king."

"*Fuck*. Your king? I won't stop, baby. You know I won't." His free hand dragged her jeans down, leaving the denim bunched beneath her backside. Working his fingers in and out of her already-clenching center, he kneaded her bottom hard, stroking in between light slaps. "Feel how sweet you are on both ends? Goddamn. Don't even get me started on your mouth. My imagination wasn't doing you justice."

A rush began at the tops of her thighs, swirling higher, unnamed muscles beginning to spasm. "Almost, *almost.*

Please keep going."

He spanked her bottom harder than before. "You think I would let you pull those jeans back up over an unsatisfied pussy?" His teeth raked up and down the side of her neck, his voice dropping as he started to sing in a tone made of gravel. Just hearing the song he'd written for her sent Jasmine's system into a tailspin. Oh God, she couldn't breathe. "I need tending, never ending. Want that, *need* that, girl in blue," he sang. His warm breath blew into Jasmine's hair, and her neck lost its ability to function, letting her head drop forward. "Grip those hips…" *Slap.* "Up into you."

Her core pulled tight, tight around his fingers. "Oh, oh… *Sarge*—"

*Slap.* "Once not enough." His thumb dragged over her clit, back again, and she climaxed. "Flipped over…round two."

Sarge caught Jasmine around the waist as her knees gave out. The sweating palms of her hands slid down the wall as she struggled to inhale. *So much. So much.* She could actually pinpoint the exact spot beneath her belly button that twisted, *twisted*, with such wicked precision, it blinded her in its perfection. Sarge was muttering husky words against the back of her neck, his body solid and reassuring behind her, keeping her anchored to reality. Although being in the darkness with a dynamic man wasn't reality for her. Never had been. Might only stick around for a short while.

Could she just enjoy it while it lasted? Without questioning it?

She wanted to so bad. When would she get this chance again?

"You with me, Jas?"

"Yeah." She managed a half smile as Sarge turned her around in his arms, those blue eyes analyzing her face like a hot, mussed-up mad scientist. "Yeah, I'm just…yeah."

The corner of his mouth lifted, forming a dimple in his

right cheek. "You like me singing to you, baby?"

*Oh damn.* Who was this sexy and adorable at the same time? Jasmine went ahead and let her knees give out again. Just so Sarge could catch her. Which he did, looking more than a little startled. It was a silly thing to do—and she didn't care. It felt really freaking good.

"*Jasmine.*" His alarm eased when he saw her smile. "I'm not even going to ask because it got me holding you again."

After a long moment of scary hesitation, Jasmine gave in to the urge to put her arms around his neck, inhale his scent. "Yeah, I like you singing to me."

Sarge jerked her up against him so hard, her feet almost left the ground. "We have some time before that retirement party tonight." A beat passed. "Hang out with me for a while?"

Jasmine didn't look. She simply leaped, along with her heart. "Okay."

# Chapter Eleven

Sarge rested his hand on the small of Jasmine's back, wanting to sing "We Are the Champions" when she didn't pull away.

It couldn't have been this easy, right? He orders some pizzas and pays everyone's factory salary for a couple hours — and in return, Jasmine agrees to spend time with him? For now, she appeared to have set aside her reservations and given them an afternoon free of the million-dollar question. *What happens now?* If Sarge thought his answer wouldn't dissolve the beautiful smile from Jasmine's face and replace it with censure, he would have told her. Straight up.

What happens now? Now he fought for her.

Sarge held no illusions that everything had been solved last night. Or back in the factory's dark machine room. Nor was he arrogant enough to believe sex would eventually change her mind for good. But he could see a crack of jagged daylight in Jasmine's wall. No longer did she have that worry in her eyes, telling Sarge exactly what she was thinking. That they were wrong together. Their age difference was too much. That people in Hook wouldn't approve. The deeply etched line between the two of them had been brushed away for now—and Sarge intended to take the crack of light in Jasmine's resolve and break it wide open.

Step one involved getting her out of Hook for a while, eliminating the worry of being seen together. Proving their relationship could be more than sweaty encounters behind locked doors. At the mall two towns over in the middle of a workday, hopefully they'd be in the clear. Notoriety was a strange thing. Some days, he could walk for hours without being recognized. Other days, not so much.

*Please let today be one of the former.*

When Sarge let his fingers dip into the waistband of Jasmine's jeans, she gifted him with one of those pursed-lip smiles. "You still haven't told me why we're at the mall."

"Two reasons." He massaged the base of her spine with his thumb, smiling when she bit her lip and groaned. "One, I need your help buying a Christmas present for Marcy."

Her brown eyes went soft. "Oh. And what's the second reason?"

"I owe you a dress."

Jasmine's back went straight. "You're not buying me clothes."

"Yeah." They reached the glass double doors of the mall's main entrance, and Sarge held one open so Jasmine could go in ahead. "I kind of figured you wouldn't be thrilled about that idea."

"So you drove me here before telling me."

"Hear me out." A group of teenage guys were pointing at him, so he threw them a casual wave, but kept Jasmine walking. "I'm going to buy you the ugliest dress we can find."

"Oh, well *now* I'm on board." Her widening smile ruined the effect of her sarcasm, spreading across her face and making her glow. "Is there more to this plan or does it end with me making Hook's worst-dressed list?"

*Damn.* Damn, he should have just taken her home. He could be kissing her mouth, her stomach, her knees. Now they were stuck in a public place and she couldn't stop being amazing for even a little while. "There's more." Sarge noticed the group of teenagers had turned and begun following them, holding up their cell phone cameras to take pictures. "You get to buy me something ugly, too."

Jasmine appeared thoughtful. "Which will take care of your guilt for ruining my dress, I don't have to feel like I owe you money, *and* we get to out-ugly each other."

"See how that works?" Feeling protective of Jasmine, even though it was only a group of kids following them, Sarge wrapped his arm around her waist and drew her close. "I'm not going to lie, a significant part of the plan involves watching you try on dresses. Ugly ones."

"Long ones. Modest ones."

"The plan said nothing about long or modest."

She laughed into his shoulder, and his chest almost caved in. His imagination conjured an image of a dozen invisible arms reaching out, trying to snatch up the details of that moment. Jasmine's warm breath passing through his sleeve, the way she lifted on her toes to press her mouth to him. Her golden scent. *God*, her scent. There had to be a way to take moments and freeze them forever, right? It didn't seem fair they had to end, like an album track. And damn, he needed to bring his thoughts down a notch before he did something crazy. Like promising to write her a never-ending song. Or begging her to laugh into his shoulder again. Or both.

"So who's going first?" Sarge managed, his voice gruff.

Her gaze lit on something up ahead. "You first. Definitely you."

Almost afraid to look, Sarge spotted the mall kiosk boasting custom tie-dyed shirts. "Oh wow. It's like they saw us coming."

Jasmine tugged him toward the booth. "Funny how plans backfire."

Twenty minutes later, Sarge was the reluctant owner of a hot-pink and baby-blue tie-dyed shirt that said "Band Geek" across the chest. Looking adorably pleased with herself, Jasmine still hadn't noticed the group of people forming across the mall, watching them and snapping pictures. Wanting to keep it that way lest she worry about them ending up on the internet, Sarge kept her facing away from the building group, throwing them an occasional smile over her head, hoping they would lose interest.

Old News traveled with light security on the road, mostly for Lita's safety, but today marked the first time Sarge had to worry about someone in his care—Jasmine—being affected by curious fans. Any other time, he wouldn't hesitate to sign autographs or take pictures, but he was all too aware that this hiatus with Jasmine was set to expire. One of her parameters had been to keep their relationship a secret. Dozens of people seeing them together would break the spell for sure.

Dammit, he hadn't been careful enough.

"All right, smart-ass. You're up," Sarge muttered, throwing the bag containing his new shirt over one shoulder. "Payback is going to be beautiful."

"I thought *ugly* was the point." Jasmine shook her head at Sarge, even as he took her hand. "You don't even remember your own rules."

Wanting to get her off the mall's main floor, Sarge pulled her into the first women's clothing store they passed. Which thankfully, turned out to be exactly what he'd had in mind. Designed for shoppers on a budget, the hemlines were brief, the material thin…and there was an overabundance of animal print. Last-minute clubbing outfits. "This makes my job pretty easy," Sarge murmured, noting they were the only customers in the store. *Thank God.* The longer they could fly under the radar, the better.

"Put me in zebra print and die."

Forcing a laugh, even though his throat was tightening with dread, Sarge's gaze snagged on a red dress with no sleeves, the number 69 in giant yellow letters below the neckline. "Oh, I think we have a winner."

Following his line of sight, Jasmine's jaw fell. "No. No way. Don't you dare."

"You were so smug with your tie-dye." Dodging her attempts to prevent him from retrieving the dress, Sarge managed to snatch it off the rack. Jasmine made for the exit, but Sarge hauled her back with an arm across her middle before she'd taken two steps. "Oh no, you don't. We had a deal. You at least have to try it on."

Jasmine wiggled in his hold, which presented a problem since her bottom was curved into his lap. Her struggle was halfhearted at best, but the way his body responded was the exact opposite of halfhearted. "Now look what you've done," Sarge rasped into her ear, thankful they were hidden by the clothing racks.

"You weren't kidding…" Jasmine breathed. "About needing me more."

"No, I wasn't. I need you all the fucking time, baby." Sarge slid a hand down her belly, pressing her back against him more firmly, groaning when she tweaked her hips. "*Jesus*. Stop doing that."

She tossed a crafty look over her shoulder. "I'll stop when you put the dress down."

"God, you play dirty." Sarge unglued their bodies with an inward groan, unable to remove his attention from her hips and thighs. "Fine. I won't make you try on the dress. But you *do* realize you're giving a man from New Jersey bragging rights?"

That brought Jasmine up short. She swayed toward the

exit, then circled back around with a glare. "Oh, fine. I'll try it on."

On their way to the dressing room, they signaled the salesperson, but she didn't even look up from her cell phone, simply waving them back. A quick glance toward the exit told Sarge the crowd following them didn't appear inclined to enter the store; however, they would most likely be waiting when he and Jasmine left. Worry over her reaction began to weigh heavier on Sarge's shoulders as he watched Jasmine disappear behind the last in a row of hanging curtains.

When she peeked through the curtain a minute later, laughter making her eyes sparkle, he forgot to be nervous. Couldn't hear a single thing over the organ knocking against his ribs. "That bad?"

"Worse."

Sarge was already on his feet moving toward the changing room. No way was he letting this opportunity pass. Not when Jasmine might try to split when she saw they'd attracted a crowd. *Christ, don't let that happen.* His good times on the road always felt forced or fleeting. Each minute of these stolen hours with Jasmine were valuable. Easy, too. So often, Sarge was required to put on a show. Be the entertaining front man for everyone present, even in his downtime. Jasmine seemed content being with him, just as he was. Or the guy he had been, before the road buried him, leaving him struggling for oxygen.

And yeah, he'd been infatuated with Jasmine as far back as he could remember. He saw her through a different lens now, though. An adult lens that clicked a little more into focus the more time they spent together. He noticed things that hadn't been apparent to his younger self. Her honesty. Her loyalty. The way she weighed his words before responding, instead of spitting out some patented response. Women like Jasmine didn't come around...ever.

Ignoring her muttered protests, Sarge tugged aside the dressing room curtain and slipped inside. "*Goddamn.*" His voice emerged ragged. "How'd you make that thing look so good?"

Good was an understatement. Had words been invented yet to describe how Jasmine's body looked, outlined in tight red fabric? She looked indecent. Unfit for public. It was the type of outfit worn to entice a man from the living room to bed—not an outfit worn dancing. Not under his watch. "This is a shirt, Sarge. Not a dress." She tugged on the hem with a laugh. "I think this means you lose."

"Hell no, baby." Taking her wrist, Sarge spun her around to face the full-length mirror. He lifted and locked her hands around the back of his neck, making the hem slip even higher. High enough for her shiny gold thong to peek out. "I definitely won."

"Sarge—" His name came out sounding breathless, Jasmine's head tipping to the side as Sarge's tongue raked up her exposed neck. "Stop turning me into moaning, weak-kneed girl. I've never been her."

"*Good.* And I can't stop." Sarge tucked a hand beneath the shirt's hem and drifted it up her bare stomach, circling her belly button with his middle finger. "Not when you keep turning me into the guy who tries to fuck through your clothes in public."

In the mirror, he watched an out-of-breath Jasmine push up on her toes to get closer, calf muscles and thighs flexing. "God, it's like I want you to. Even though I know it's a bad idea."

His growing cock stretched the material of his boxer briefs with such a swift rush of sensation, Sarge had to strangle a groan. The hand beneath Jasmine's dress moved higher to knead her full breasts. "The cops would understand, right? Once they showed up and saw you in that—" He broke off, jealousy coating his vision in green as their gazes locked in the mirror. "Forget I said that. This is only for me."

Jasmine nodded, mouth falling open on a gasp when he thumbed her pointed nipples, back and forth. Her legs were squeezing together, obviously trying to ease an ache between her thighs, a predicament he understood all too well. Her dark hair was spread out on his chest, those brown eyes shining, her skin glowing.

"*Dammit,* Jasmine. Do you have any idea how gorgeous you are?" Sarge turned her around for a kiss he needed to avoid certain death. "I thought I knew. But now you're actually seeing me and I didn't…I had no idea. Your eyes…"

When she clung to his shoulders and not only allowed his tongue to plunder her mouth, but responded with hot, equal measure, Sarge knew he had to break away. Or as sure as they were standing there, he'd be thrusting inside her tight body in under a minute, covering her mouth as she bounced up and down against the dressing room wall. Already his need seeped from the head of his dick, a demand for pleasure. A demand for *Jasmine.*

He had to close his eyes while catching his breath, forehead lodged in the hollow of Jasmine's neck. Couldn't look. If he saw even a hint of invitation on her face, there would be hell to pay. "I'm buying the dress. For later."

"*Fineyesokay.*"

There was a wealth of pain in his laughter, but somehow it still felt real and incredible. "I'm going to back out of here slowly and stay out. While you get dressed. In regular clothes. So I can take you somewhere private and rip them off."

She nodded, bumping into his jaw. "Sarge?"

"Yeah."

"When were you going to tell me about the crowd of people following us?"

That's when Sarge knew. He was out-of-his-mind, flat-on-his-ass in love with Jasmine. Not like it had been before. Not just an attraction or an overdeveloped crush that bred more frustration than satisfaction. No, this…this feeling burned inside his stomach like a bonfire being fed with kerosene. His impulse was to hide out in the dressing room forever, snarling at anyone who came within ten feet of her. And at the same time, he wanted to stick her up on his shoulders and walk the streets, shouting at anyone who would listen how fucking incredible she was.

"I…" He swallowed and pulled away, unable to resist smoothing Jasmine's hair back. Their respite from Hook was coming to an end too damn quickly. "I thought you didn't see them."

Her shoulders lifted and fell as she stepped away, already retrieving her clothes. "It's okay. I don't recognize any of them from Hook. If anyone in town sees the pictures…." He mourned the loss of her legs as denim hid them from view. "They know we're just friends."

The bonfire in Sarge's stomach hissed. "Yeah. Just two friends shopping together, right?" Jasmine's head lifted at his tone, her sweet mouth already opening to remind him they were a secret. But if she said the words now, minutes after she'd trapped his heart in a cage, he wouldn't handle it well. His counterargument would be the furthest thing from reasonable, and this free afternoon she'd given him would be a waste. The alternative was to stay on his game and not ruin the moment by pushing.

Easier said than done, but he'd swallow the irritation knowing it would keep something real with Jasmine within reach.

"I'll wait outside," Sarge said before she could speak. As he grabbed up the discarded 69 dress from the floor with the clear intention to purchase it, he winked up at her. "We'll call the contest a tie."

# Chapter Twelve

You're not getting rid of me that easily.

Had it only been this morning Sarge had issued that warning in her kitchen? Apparently he'd been serious as a heart attack, because he wouldn't budge. Worse, despite her attempt to create distance, the idea of Sarge budging made her stomach plummet. But just *look* at what his attention was doing to her.

As they walked side by side through the mall, toward their final stop to buy a toy, Jasmine felt a confidence that had been absent for years. Instead of her usual impulse to twist her hair up into a bun, it was hanging loose around her shoulders in messy waves. She'd applied lipstick before leaving the dressing room and couldn't remember ever having been so aware of her mouth because of the way Sarge continued to stare down at it, as if imagining its various erotic uses. There was a new lightness twisting and turning through her limbs, making her want to dance. Or climb Sarge's body, knowing— *knowing*—his reaction would be *fuck yes*, no matter where they were or who was watching.

So. *Deep breath*. It wasn't just confidence in herself. It was confidence in Sarge. That's what had spooked her back in the clothing store. That's what allowed the doubt bubble to inflate and pop in the form of verbal sabotage. This experience with Sarge had started as physical but in a short space of time had turned…serious. There had been no formal discussion—hell, she'd just reminded him they were only "friends"—but lip service didn't stop the pull between them from strengthening.

If he left tomorrow, there would be a gap. A big, funny, sweet, dirty gap where Sarge had made his presence known. She would turn thirty the day after Christmas and he would be back in Los Angeles, surrounded by better, more successful…*younger* options. So this was where Jasmine had to make a decision. And really, there was only one decision to make, because Sarge *would* leave. Little by little, she needed to insert tiny air pockets between them until he stopped being so reachable. So Sarge.

As if he knew her exact thoughts, Sarge sighed and put an arm around her shoulders, leading her into the toy store. Pop stars shrieked from the speakers, putting their own spin on classic Christmas songs. Unlike the rest of the mall, this store was packed full of parents making purchases for the big day. They were putting the Santa hat–clad employees through their paces, sending them into the back room looking for toys that couldn't be found on the floor.

Sarge tugged Jasmine into the warmth of his body to avoid robots demonstrating their skills in front of a colorful display. It was on the tip of her tongue to remind him of the cell phone cameras documenting their every move from just outside the store, but Sarge released her before she got the chance.

"All right." He circled the robot display. "Marcy was disappointed I wasn't small enough to hold in a blanket. Think maybe she'd like baby dolls?"

"Dolls…plural? How many were you planning on buying her?"

Sarge propped both hands on his hips to survey the store and nodded once. "All of them."

It took Jasmine a moment to speak around the insistent tug in her chest. "Let's look a little more. Marcy has quite a few dolls." Jasmine could feel Sarge following close behind her as they wound through a busy aisle. She missed his arm around her shoulders so much, she felt chilled. "Um. Marcy loves dinosaurs." Jasmine picked up a *Jurassic World* figurine set, complete with buildings to destroy. "This could be fun. It even has the T. rex—that's her favorite."

Sarge rubbed his chin. "You sure it won't scare her?"

Jasmine thought of the spunky three-year-old hurling herself off River's couch onto a pillow fort. "She doesn't scare easily."

"Okay." Sarge stepped back, eyeing the shelves. "Let's get them all."

Her laughter turned heads, so she ducked behind his big frame. "You can't just show up with hundreds of boxes," she whispered. "Your sister will kill you. And me by association."

His throat muscles slid up and down. "I wasn't in Hook for Marcy's first three Christmases. I have to make up for it somehow, right?"

At once, she couldn't breathe. Sarge was doing his best to hide the guilt, but it was there in the set of his jaw, the heaviness behind his eyes. It took every molecule of her willpower not to throw herself into his arms and cling. Cling for dear life. Because who could ever top this man? He was everything at once. Good, strong, thoughtful…bad when he needed to be. More, he was harboring pain. Keeping it close so it wouldn't touch anyone else.

"Sarge. You'll make up for it without the toys. Just being here *now* is enough…" Even as she reassured him, an idea occurred. "Actually, hold on."

Jasmine dodged two children having a sword fight and ducked into an unoccupied aisle, two away from where they'd discovered the dinosaurs. Sarge joined her there a moment later, curiosity painting his expression. "What is it?"

Surprised he hadn't seen the child-sized guitars yet, Jasmine realized it was due to his total focus on her. His gaze moved over her face, lighting on her cheeks, hair, lips. Tapping into her reserve of strength, Jasmine tore her attention from Sarge, went up on her toes, and unhooked the guitar from its hanging place. "I was thinking you could teach Marcy to play." Brow furrowed, he took the offered guitar, but didn't say anything. Jasmine immediately wanted to recall the suggestion. With it, she'd called attention to the four-hundred-pound gorilla in the room. That Sarge would most likely be accepting the new contract. And leaving. "Even when you're on the road, there are webcams. Skype. People learn to play instruments through the internet all the time now. I just thought—"

"It's perfect, Jas." He reached out and cupped a hand over her mouth. "It's perfect, and no more talking about me leaving. Deal? Nothing else is worth thinking about when I've got you standing in front of me."

When Jasmine felt her legs bump the shelves, she realized his words had literally made her stagger. But she couldn't respond because his hand covered her mouth. Her body, however, responded quite readily when he crowded closer, pulse whirring, tummy tightening, toes stretching inside her shoes. Some vestige of consciousness had her saying his name, but it came out muffled in his palm.

"I changed my mind," he murmured. "We're going to talk right now because who knows when I'll get another chance. And no matter how this conversation goes, it's going to end with me kissing the hell out of you in this toy store. You with me?"

No idea what was coming, but positive it would be a major, mother-effing game changer, Jasmine started to shake her head—

"Um. Excuse me… Sarge Purcell from Old News, right?"

As if he'd heard the same question four million times, Sarge nodded without even looking at their intruder. His head tipped forward on an exhale that ruffled her hair, remaining that way for long moments. When he finally straightened, Jasmine saw a different side of Sarge. The rock band front man. His smile was just the right amount of cocky, sprinkled with a hint of self-deprecation. With an apologetic look intended solely for her, he turned to greet the newcomer— and drew up short.

Curious, Jasmine followed his line of sight to find Sarge's snowballing group of admirers climbing over each other to get a look at them. They moved farther and farther into the store, jamming into every corner with the slightest bit of room, speaking in excited tones. Sarge moved in front of Jasmine, wedging her back against the toy shelf. "Hey, guys." A flash went off. "Happy holidays. Do you mind—"

"Play something!"

Sarge shifted, reaching back to brush a thumb over her hand. A reassurance. "I don't have my guitar. But if someone has a pen, I can—"

He broke off when everyone laughed. "You're holding a guitar," a man toward the front pointed out. "Come on. It's Christmas."

"Right." Sarge threw her a glance over his shoulder as everyone started to clap, slow at first, then picking up speed. Jasmine expected him to make another excuse or play the crowd something quick, but what he said next completely took her off guard. "I'll play something if my…friend here agrees to sing with me."

"Sarge. *No*," Jasmine whispered against his back, heaviness crowding in her throat. "They're not asking to hear *me* sing."

"They'll change their minds once you start," he returned, with total conviction. "You're one of the best singers I've ever heard, Jas."

Drawing air grew almost impossible. How had this trip to the mall turned into a tour of her insecurities? "I haven't sung in so long. I'm not sure I even can anymore."

Sarge held up a finger to the onlookers and faced her. When one large hand started to reach for her hip, but dropped on the trip over, she realized what an effort he made not to touch her while others were looking. A restriction *she'd* placed on him.

"Sarge."

"*Hey*." The importance behind that single word held her in thrall. "I started playing my guitar because of you, Jasmine. That day you sang in the blue dress? I had to make music after that because you made it sound so good. Made it look like a necessity."

The floor disappeared beneath her feet, leaving her hovering over nothing. "You never told me that."

A twinkle replaced the seriousness in his gaze. "Maybe I was waiting for us to be standing in a mall toy store full of strangers." His eyebrows dipped, head tilting in the most persuasive manner she'd ever witnessed. "Sing with me."

She studied the anxious group beyond his shoulder, wondering if she'd lost her damn mind. Any other Friday, she would still be working in the factory. Getting ready for a nowhere date or making plans to do happy hour at the Third Shift. How had she gotten here? "Okay," she breathed before she could stop to question to decision.

One corner of Sarge's mouth lifted, his pride drawing her forward so they could face their makeshift audience side by side. Much like the day she'd sung at the Feast of San Gennaro, her stomach pinched with tightening knots…but it wasn't unpleasant. It was anticipation. And when Sarge strummed the first few chords of "Joyful, Joyful," she couldn't stop the smile from spreading across her face.

• • •

Jasmine threw the car into park a couple blocks from the Third Shift, her vision beginning to blur with mirthful tears.

"Did you see the disappointment on that woman's face when I wasn't Jon Bon Jovi?" Sarge's imitation of the crestfallen woman sent Jasmine back into a fit of laughter. "She actually wanted me dead. She already purchased a Sarge Purcell voodoo doll and covered it in pins."

"You can't really blame her," Jasmine said, wiping her eyes. "We were only a few minutes from Bon Jovi's house. He probably draws a crowd when he goes out."

He lunged across the console to tickle her ribs. "I can't believe you're taking her side. Some singing partner you turned out to be."

"I'm sorry!" she squealed.

"Sorry about what?"

Jasmine twisted, trying to get away from his torturous fingers and failing. "I'm going solo. Sorry you had to find out this way."

Sarge's gaze narrowed. "Oh, baby. Now you're going to get it." His big hands planted on her denim-clad thighs, squeezing the most ticklish spot on her body. Jasmine shot up with a yelp, legs shooting apart to dislodge his hand to no avail. She couldn't pinpoint the exact second his touch went from playful to downright sexual, but instead of tickling, Sarge began massaging the insides of her thighs. Pushed close to kiss a path over her ear.

"One hour, Jas," he rasped. "One hour at this party before I take you home."

"What happens at home?" Jasmine breathed, knowing full well she played a dangerous game. He'd made his intentions for the evening abundantly clear every chance he'd gotten since leaving the toy store. Backing her into alcoves, kissing her against the driver's side door so long she'd been panting when he finished. This thing between her and Sarge was flat-out insane. She couldn't catch her breath, couldn't seem to stop turning up the volume on their attraction. Even as common sense told her to back off, her body—and God, maybe even her heart—had gone deaf to her protests.

"What happens at home?" Sarge's bulk loomed closer, cornering her in the driver's side seat, as his fingers yanked down her jeans zipper. When he reached inside to cup the apex of her thighs, Jasmine whimpered and allowed her legs to fall wider. "When we get home I've got this edge to take off. Soon as I make sure you're wet enough, your feet won't be touching the floor again for a goddamn while." Sarge's fist ground down on her center, same time as his teeth clamped on the flesh of her shoulder. He growled, biting down *just* enough, before drawing back with a soothing lick. "You *will* get off, because that's a huge part of what gets me off. But, baby, it's going to feel like I'm just using your little body. Using the fuck out of it."

Oh God, she could come just this way. His rasping voice in her ear, his rough palm dragging back and forth over her clit. "Yes, I want that. I want you to use me."

His uneven exhale heated her cleavage. "That right? You want a desperate man riding your pussy from the back, so hot to come he forgets he's a lot stronger than you? Forgets what gentle means?"

Jasmine's most sensitive flesh clenched like a fist. A prolonged, devastating squeeze. "Oh my God, *yes*."

"*Good.*" With a clear effort, Sarge zipped her pants back up, heaving himself back into the passenger seat. "One hour," he said, wiping sweat from his upper lip as Jasmine tried to regain some semblance of control on the driver's side.

She opened the door a crack, allowing cool air to infiltrate the steamy car. Still, it took long minutes for her temperature to lower, her breathing to calm. "I want to leave with you tonight, Sarge. You didn't have to guarantee it like that."

"No?" Sarge's jaw flexed, his closed fist tapping the passenger door. "I have to walk into the Third Shift and behave like we're just friends. Things might not look the same an hour from now."

Although his explanation was vague, Jasmine discerned his meaning. The Third Shift had a way of moving pawns around on the Hook chessboard, as if the dingy establishment had some mystical quality. She and Sarge had gotten along fine until now under the restrictions she'd placed on their relationship, because they hadn't *been* around anyone who knew them, apart from River. Once they walked through the barroom door, their temporary hiatus from acknowledging the pitfalls of their relationship would be over.

Sarge exited the car and rounded the front bumper, pulling Jasmine's door open fully and offering her a hand. "Will you let me buy your drinks?" He brushed his fingers over her cheek. "Give me *something*, baby."

It felt a little like signing over her independence, which she didn't like, but it seemed a small price to pay to put him at ease. Not to mention, you could drink all night in the Third Shift and fail to rack up a bill higher than forty dollars. "Okay."

She allowed Sarge to help her from the car, meeting his eyes when he didn't immediately let go of her hand. He didn't say anything, simply looking down at her, his brow furrowed. When he released Jasmine from his grip, he immediately tried to take it back, but she moved out of his reach toward the bar.

Every step she took felt unsteady, blood ticking in her temples. Had someone knit a bowling ball into her stomach lining? Feeling Sarge at her back, Jasmine swallowed her nerves and walked into the Third Shift, already feeling the distance between them. Hating it, but knowing it was necessary all the same.

One step inside and already she wanted to dive back out into the freezing night. Into Sarge's hold. And he *would* hold her, take her home, kiss away all the doubt. A cheer went up when the regulars spotted the local hero in their midst and that was it. They were separated by the shifting crowd. Someone took her coat and threw it on the usual huge pile over the waitress station. Hands patted her shoulders, familiar faces kissed her cheeks in greeting, as if they hadn't seen each other at work that afternoon. She twisted in the crowd to find Sarge. How had so many people managed to get between them already? His height made him visible in the sea of partygoers and his gaze remained steady on her, distracting her from the conversation she'd been thrust into without preamble.

River popped up to her right, nursing what Jasmine knew to be a Diet Coke. "Hey! You disappeared on me earlier. I had to fend off this rowdy pack of pizza scavengers on my own."

"I know. I'm sorry, I…" A lie sat poised on Jasmine's tongue, but she choked it down. They were always honest with each other. That wouldn't stop now. "I was with Sarge, but I didn't expect to just leave like that. I should have called you."

One of the bartenders ambled between them, a bucket of ice balanced on his head, but Jasmine could feel her best friend weighing what she'd said. "You were with Sarge." River sipped through her straw until she reached the bottom of her drink. "You know, my brother was responsible for the early dismissal today."

"I pieced it together," Jasmine said, spying the man in

question across the bar. His stunt that afternoon had clearly earned him new admirers. Men still dressed in their factory finest were slapping him on the back, shoving icy bottles of Budweiser into his hand. There were women, too. Young women asking to take pictures with him, tossing their hair around the way people wave flags. A worm of jealousy crawled inside Jasmine, but she ordered it to get lost. On some faraway planet, where Sarge could become her boyfriend, he would be faithful. Unlike the men she'd dated before, her belief in his honesty was unshakable. How odd to have that kind of conviction in a man so young. But character didn't evolve over time, did it? Sarge's had always been there, always been intact.

"Everyone was asking me why he didn't show up to his own party. I thought he was just being Sarge. You know, doing good things and not taking credit," River continued, following Jasmine's gaze. "Now I'm wondering if he pulled that whole thing off just to spend time with you."

*Dios*, Jasmine wished for a drink so she'd have something to do with her hands. "No, he didn't. That's crazy."

River's regard didn't waver. "How serious is it, Jas?"

The crowd seemed to get louder around her, elbows bumping, raucous laughter grating along her senses. "We just went to the mall," she answered lamely, in the understatement of the year. "He...I sang. *We* sang for people at the mall."

Her friend's expression fell, as if Jasmine had imparted news of a major catastrophe. "Sarge got you to sing?"

Jasmine's nod was jerky. She'd put on blinders to the importance of what took place in the toy store that afternoon, but having some breathing room from Sarge forced the pretense to drop. River knew too well that Jasmine hadn't sung in years. Her voice had faded along with hope, a little more with every rejection. Sarge might not even realize what he'd done today, but he'd empowered Jasmine to take back what she'd allowed nameless faces to steal. God, she'd never felt more like herself she had since Sarge came back to Hook. Maybe Jasmine should have been thrilled with the resurgence of confidence, but she wasn't. Not when the man who'd held up a mirror and forced her to look at herself would be gone in a matter of days.

"Hey," River prompted, worry plain on her face. "Is this… are you going to be okay?"

"Yeah. *Yes*." Someone pressed a drink into Jasmine's hand, and she took it partly on reflex, but mostly out of gratefulness to have a distraction from her best friend's scrutiny. "He's leaving, right? It'll take care of itself."

When River's blue eyes squeezed shut, Jasmine knew in her bones that Sarge stood behind her. Had been the one to bring her a drink. Jasmine wanted to sprint for the ladies' room, but remained rooted to the ground. Sarge drew up beside her—not touching—and leaned over to kiss River's cheek. "Hey, Riv." His voice was strained. "Marcy with the sitter?"

"Yes." River split a look between them before checking her watch. "My time is almost up, though. Fifteen minutes more and I'll turn into a pumpkin."

"You sure you're heading home?" Sarge asked, his usual smile looking forced.

Jasmine watched with curiosity as her friend's shoulders drooped. "W-where else would I be going?"

Sarge gave a slow headshake. "Nowhere. Let me get you a cab."

"Already called one. See you both tomorrow." River gave them both a hurried peck on the cheek, waving over her shoulder as the crowd swallowed her up.

"What was that about?" Jasmine asked, wondering what the hell she'd been missing. Had she been so caught up in the force that was Sarge, she'd let her best friend duties fall by the wayside? Unacceptable. "Sarge?"

He tipped back his Budweiser, throat working as he swallowed the hearty sip. "I stopped by the church today to see Adeline. She told me River has been working night shifts at some club."

"*What?*"

"I take it you didn't know, either." He cast a glance toward the door where River exited. "Did you know Vaughn isn't even aware of Marcy? River is doing all of this on her own and there might not be a need for it. He could help."

Jasmine's pulse slowed. "That was your sister's decision, Sarge. You need to speak with her about it. Unless…it's too late and you've already done something you can't take back."

Blue eyes bored into hers. "I had to. Not everything takes care of itself."

The bowling ball tugging on Jasmine's stomach lining gained around ten pounds when Sarge repeated the words she'd just said to River. About him. Somehow since walking into the bar, she'd disappointed two people who mattered like hell to her. "I'm sorry you heard that, but you're taking it the wrong way."

His laughter was devoid of humor. "There's only one way to take it, Jas. This arrangement works for you because I'm getting gone. No muss, no fuss. No one in town the wiser." He set his empty beer bottle down on one of the wobbly bar tables, exerting enough force to turn a couple heads. "That was the deal up front, though, wasn't it? *Nothing* changed along the way."

The way he said it suggested everything had changed. He knew it. He knew Jasmine knew it, too. Knew it deep in her gut that orange flickers had flamed into a fire. Instead of admitting the facts, though, self-preservation rose up and snatched the opportunity to protect her. "I was convenient for you, too." She whispered for his ears alone. "It went both ways."

"*Convenient.*" The word came out sounding choked. He took a step away from her, as if ending their conversation, but he came right back, eyes shooting sparks. She expected him to stop closing in, but he didn't. Just kept coming until his breath was pelting her forehead. "You know, I actually thought I could get you out of my blood with a few nights in bed. But it was a goddamn fool's mission. *I'm* the fool. I'll admit that. Nothing will ever work—because *you're in me.* And there's nothing convenient about it."

"Sarge—"

"I saw this coming. We're in this fucking place ten minutes and you're already talking about us in the past tense. What happened?"

She needed to step back before Sarge overwhelmed her. A voice in her head urged her toward him. *Just leap. Just leap.* Even in a bar full of people who would judge her, laugh at her for preying on a younger man. A man who'd earned all the glory she'd been so vocal about and confident she would obtain. Who cared, though, as long as he walked out beside her?

Those were dangerous thoughts. Thoughts that would lead her down a path to heartbreak. She'd be the only one left behind to field the fallout. "I need to use the bathroom," she managed, backing away, a little surprised when Sarge let her go. With his determined face fresh and unfading in her mind, Jasmine leaned over the bathroom sink, the bass from the bar stereo matching her pumping heartbeat. There was a sense of impending doom in the atmosphere, and she couldn't swim free of it. She just needed a night to sleep it off and face the Sarge situation with fresh eyes in the morning. Resolved to give Sarge her apartment keys, then call a cab to River's— alone—Jasmine took a deep breath and left the bathroom.

Sarge was waiting in the dimness of the hallway. For a

split second, Jasmine considered staying the course, walking the opposite direction toward the bar, instead of toward the bar's back party room where Sarge stood. Waiting. His jaw was carved from granite, chest rising and falling with fast breaths. *Dammit*, he was pulling her in, beckoning her closer without even moving or speaking. But the need in his eyes spoke volumes. Sarge was as desperate as Jasmine was for oblivion, and it would only require taking a few steps to achieve it.

He tilted his head, pain evident in his voice. "Baby."

*No stopping it.* She couldn't even think past getting to him, jogging down the dark corridor and being caught up against his sturdy body. Before their mouths even met, one male hand tangled in her hair, drawing her in. Her legs twined around his waist because they couldn't *not*. Without that intimacy between their bodies, she would capsize, sink, bottom out.

Sarge took a few uneven steps backward as their mouths feasted, bumping against the push-bar leading to the party room. And then they were in the unoccupied space, strewn with chairs and banquet tables. He unraveled her hair from his fist long enough to shove a metal chair under the door handle, barring anyone entrance. "Won't leave with me, huh?" His palm slapped down on her bottom, making Jasmine break the kiss on a gasp, even as her legs tightened around his hips. "Did you think that would stop me, Jas?"

Jasmine was suffocating without his kiss, but he only nipped at her mouth, pulling back before she could get the real thing. "*Sarge.*"

"Answer me. Did you think I would rest until we got here tonight?" Another tug of her bottom lip with his teeth. "Wasn't even sure I could get through an *hour* without our skin touching. Then all those hands on you, eyes on you. *Goddammit.* I have to fuck you, baby. Don't you know how bad I need to fuck you? *Answer* me."

He dropped her backside onto something cold and metal.

She could only remove her focus from him long enough to find herself propped on the tray rest of an empty buffet station. "Yes. I *know*."

"You can't know." He slid his hands up her thighs, shoved them apart with a growl. Snapping blue eyes focused on her core, his big, blunt-fingered hands unzipping his jeans, pulling the zipper lower, lower...to reveal his ready male flesh. Jasmine's breath caught as Sarge shoved down the hindering denim and took the almost cumbersome erection in his hand with a groan. "All for one woman. She can do this to me just by breathing. Putting on lip balm. Laughing. Singing. Pulling her hair back. Does that sound *convenient* to you?"

Jasmine was trembling head to toe, but managed to shake her head. That response didn't satisfy Sarge—or this *amped-up* version of Sarge, rather, that loomed above her, stroking his flesh and looking her over. Hungry, so hungry, to feel his most private pulse beating in her palm, she reached out to replace his hand. Before she could satisfy the urge, Sarge gripped Jasmine's hips and hauled her off the buffet, spinning her around a second later to wrench the jeans down her body.

Open mouth moving through her hair, his harsh breaths heated her scalp. "I'm going to show you convenient. When we're done, you'll think convenient means well-fucked by Sarge." He lifted Jasmine with an arm around the waist to remove her jeans fully, kicking them aside and setting her back down. His casual show of strength sent her belly into a series of backflips, releasing a flow of warmth between her thighs. She pressed her bottom back into his lap, silk thong against hard flesh, purring when he reached around to fondle her.

Jasmine planted her hands on the metal rack and looked back at Sarge, watching his eyes glaze over at the way she moved, swaying and popping her hips like a private dancer. "Can I have you like this, *mi rey*?"

"I'm your king again, am I? No. You can't have it yet." He fit his erection into the valley of her bottom and bucked. Hard. "Not until you need a pump of my dick so bad, you're clawing at my ass like a trapped wildcat."

Jasmine was still moaning at the imagery of that when Sarge turned her again, already applying the condom to his arousal. She pitched right on unsteady legs, but Sarge caught her elbow, dragging her into the heat of his body. The desperation radiating from him was so thick, she moved without conscious thought, lifting his T-shirt to lick his abdomen, his pectorals. "*Please*, I want you."

"Good, baby. You're about to take me." His promise still hung in the air when Sarge scooped Jasmine off the ground, one arm banded around the small of her back. The move dragged her body up his arousal, stopping when it met the apex of her legs, its weight settling against the inside of her thigh. Anticipation blinded Jasmine, but she could feel his touch slide down her buttocks, felt him guiding his erection right where she welcomed it with damp heat. His chest absorbed Jasmine's throaty scream as he filled her in one savage upward jerk of his hips.

Craving leverage, craving movement, Jasmine expected Sarge to back her up into the buffet and give it to her hard. But he didn't. Instead, he bent his knees just slightly, making it possible to stand on her barest tiptoes. Gone was every ounce of sweetness from Sarge, replaced with dirty, wicked lust. A hint of menace.

She tried to wrap her legs around him, climb up, seeking some kind of anchor that would give her the freedom to chase release. Satisfy them both. But Sarge shook his head, brushing their panting mouths together. "You were the first woman I ever stroked off thinking about, Jasmine. Again. And again. Until I couldn't even hear your name without locking myself in the closest room." His callused hands massaged her bottom with punishing force. "Turns out I got it right that first time, though. Didn't I? This babysitter's pussy tastes just like sugar." A savoring noise ripped from his throat. "Tight enough to strangle a man."

Jasmine's legs turned to liquid, making her slip and impale herself more fully on Sarge's length. Broken Spanish fell from her mouth. She tried once more unsuccessfully to climb Sarge's body, but he slapped her bottom for making the effort.

"Time to return the favor, Jasmine." He angled his upper half away, his heated gaze tracking down to where their bodies connected. "Stroke yourself off to *me* now. While I watch." Another rough spank of her backside, the sound so delicious they both had to close their eyes. "I won't move. But you better. Starting now. *Now*, Jasmine."

# Chapter Thirteen

Sarge felt control slipping through his fingers. Jasmine didn't deserve to be punished for his obsession. Didn't deserve to be denied the swiftest route to climax. But frustration had built inside him, snowballing from the time they'd walked into the Third Shift. How could he act normal, carry on conversations, when his hands were shaking with the need to be on Jasmine? Not just so he could hold her down and give pleasure. No. He'd wanted to walk in holding her hand. Wanted to look every man in the eye and let them know their chances with Jasmine had been knocked down to zero percent.

Being denied that right had started the bomb ticking in his stomach. But hearing the flippant way she dismissed their relationship had caused the explosion. There was a lurking sense of dread, too, but it felt too good being angry, so he ignored the warning voice calling for him to slow down. Telling him he couldn't allow shrapnel from the bomb blast to ruin the progress he'd made. Listening meant stopping, though, and it felt too good giving Jasmine a taste of what he'd endured.

"Please," she sobbed, pushing up on her toes. "I can't get high enough."

As far as Sarge was concerned, she was doing goddamn perfect. His cock was lodged in tightness; Jasmine was making these sexy whining noises every time he disallowed her legs from gaining leverage around his hips. Her fingernails were digging into his shoulders, but every time she tried to pull herself up, Sarge shook her grip loose. His light hold on her bottom kept her from falling, but it wasn't enough to seat her at a satisfying angle. And God help him, watching her struggle to get on top of his dick had him turned on to the point of pain. Good pain, though. Pain that distracted him from the one she'd created in his chest.

"Come on, baby." Sarge bent his knees just long enough for Jasmine to ride him hard for a few seconds, before straightening again, his movement dragging her back onto tiptoes. "It feels good when I'm deep, doesn't it? When you're stretching to get all of me in?"

"*Yes*," Jasmine moaned. "Please. I need more."

"You need more? *Work* for it. I can feel your clit…all wet and swollen. Rub her on me. Let her feel my tip." Sarge gave a shallow thrust of his hips. "You've made my cock hard for years, now you're going to fuck yourself on it, Jasmine. When it starts to hurt, think of me waiting until everyone was asleep on the tour bus before jerking off to a memory. Stroking so hard I couldn't breathe, thinking of that peek I got of your pussy. That's what hurt looks like. When you can only get off on something you've never had."

Sarge bit back a roar when Jasmine's fingers dug into the flesh of his ass, yanking him forward as she rolled her hips. The move inched him further into her snug pussy, while still keeping him only partially sheathed. They were locked in the dirtiest dance of all time, Jasmine working her clit against the head of his dick, her slender thighs sliding up and down his hairy, more muscular ones. "Yes, yes, yes…"

*Fuck.* He was losing his own battle now. Watching, hearing, feeling Jasmine's frantic use of his erection to masturbate herself was the hottest sight Sarge had witnessed in his life. Every few seconds, she managed to push high enough on her toes to take another inch of him. But each time, her thighs immediately shot up to get more and he'd block their progress with resolute hands. Then…Lord. She started sinking her teeth into his shoulders and chest for denying her. Started pouting in a way that made him feel like a dirty man doing bad things, making him even harder. Making his balls draw high and heavy. She started bucking like an unbroken pony, forehead digging into his chest as she moaned.

The slick slide of her pussy up and down the top third of his cock, her desperate clawing at his ass—the way she jerked him forward—grew to be too much. Jasmine might have put him through hell—most of the time without realizing it—but denying the down and dirty fucking they both required was punishing him in the process. Just a little longer…just a little so he wouldn't forget how gorgeous she looked, forget how bad she wanted him tonight.

And then she sobbed. A shuddering sound full of misery, and his heart rebelled, sinking straight down to his stomach. His hands sank into her hair, smoothing the strands and tilting her head back. When Sarge glimpsed her face, he stopped breathing. If he could see through Jasmine's eyes at that moment, he knew their surroundings would be blurry. She seemed unable to focus, her head falling back as if unhinged from her neck. There was a row of teeth marks on her bottom lip that appeared on the verge of bleeding. And the *pain* in her eyes…pain he'd caused. *No no no.*

"Please," she murmured. "I *can't*…I need—"

Sarge cut her off with his mouth, his own focus wavering at the taste of her. God. Had it been years or minutes since he kissed her? Getting enough wasn't a possibility. *Never.* Not with his mouth or his body. Groaning at the way her pussy flexed around him as their mouths wrestled for a good taste, Sarge gripped Jasmine beneath the knees and spread her legs, lifting and propping them on his hips.

Sinking down onto him—*finally*—she screamed into his mouth.

"I'm sorry. I'm sorry I made you hurt. Going to fuck it better, baby. Going to pump until you come." He walked them backward so he could reach past her hip, propping one hand on the metal buffet, supporting her ass with the other. Already she was starting to ride his cock, clinging to his upper body while grinding down on him like a goddess. "Give me a twist on the way back up—*ahhh fuck.* That's it, you tight little thing. Working my dick like a goddamn stripper pole, aren't you? You have any idea how hard I'm going to come?"

Her breath released in a hot gust at his ear. "Me first."

Sarge's laugh transformed into a deep grunt as her pace changed, grew more erratic. Jasmine's thighs were spread so wide, she was doing the splits on his lap, that fine-as-hell backside undulating on his pressing forearm. Sarge matched her fevered pace, driving himself up and into her squeezing heat, his thrusts so savage he worried he might hurt her. But she only bit his neck and whimpered for more. Not enough, though. It wasn't enough. He needed her secured somewhere so he could slam into her willing pussy and forget his own fucking name.

As if she could read his mind, she gripped his hair, leaned back and moaned. "Yes. Harder. More."

"Never stop saying that to me." Sarge pinned Jasmine's ass to the metal buffet's edge and hooked both arms beneath her knees. He took a moment to savor how she looked, breathless and begging for his assault, before ramming home. Even as she gasped his name, her body remained stationary, finally allowing his cock deep as possible. "Feel how I belong here, baby? Feel how we fit together?" Sarge rolled his hips back and rocked forward, pushing, pushing until his balls strained at her entrance. "It's never felt right before now—and you know it. No way this is wrong. No way I wasn't meant to own this part of you. *Every* fucking part."

"Yes." Jasmine breathed the word, head falling back as Sarge started to thrust. He jarred her body with each collision of their bodies, bouncing her tits inside her shirt. "Oh my *God*. So good, so good, *so good*."

Sarge's spine began to tingle, growing tight at the base. He gave an irritated headshake, pissed that his need for Jasmine continued to end their encounters too soon, although he suspected any amount of time would be too soon with her. Trying to conjure a distasteful image that might delay his oncoming climax didn't work, either. There was nothing but Jasmine in his universe. Nothing.

Craving her gorgeous brown eyes on him, needing to go over the edge together, Sarge leaned in and kissed her mouth. He drew back as the kiss's fervor increased, bringing her with him, before pulling away. Holding her attention, Sarge propped her right leg over his shoulder to free his hand. Then he licked his thumb and stroked it over her clit, holding her steady when she jerked.

"Ah God, Jasmine. You look so good with my cock sliding in and out between those legs. You know your knees shake every time I hit your limit?" He thumbed her clit, sliding back and forth over the tight nub, his hips starting to piston out of pure necessity. "That's right. Every time I find the back of your pussy, you vibrate like I hit a button."

"Again, *again*." On cue, a shiver ran through her limbs. "So close."

"Me, too. *Fuck*. Me, too." Jasmine flung her other leg over Sarge's shoulder, leaving both feet hovering, the added depth tearing a growl from his lips. "Fuck, that's tight, baby. So tight for me." This was it. He couldn't hold back. Pain between his legs. A relentless, driving, throbbing ache. "Tell me your fucking legs are up in the air because you want my come. Pout for it. Let me see that little pout."

The excitement in her eyes was almost enough to knock Sarge into oblivion, but then she frowned, teeth sinking into her bottom lip, her tits still bouncing from the force his drives. "Please, please, Sarge. *Ay que rico.* I want it inside m-me."

She climaxed on the final word and Sarge sprinted after, their wet, spasming flesh slapping together as strangled moans rent the air. Oxygen eluded him…he couldn't pull enough into his lungs. A series of images flashed on the backs of his eyelids. The first time he'd met Jasmine in his living room and spent the night wondering about her. Jasmine laughing as she jumped off the community pool diving board. Jasmine singing beside him at the mall, her voice clear and rich. She was it for him. Always had been. His head buzzed and spun with urgency. On the heels of an orgasm that had stripped the remains of his filter, Sarge could process only one fact. If he didn't keep her, he'd never be happy a day in his life. Not now. Not after knowing and loving her at this stage of his life. Solidifying what he'd always known.

"I love you, Jasmine." His body deflated against her as the words were released. Relief. So much relief at finally saying them. Getting them out of his chest where they'd been held prisoner for so long. They meant more now, though. This wasn't a crush or an infatuation—every minute in her company confirmed it. He'd loved Jasmine *then* and he loved her more *now*. "I've always, *always* loved you. I'm not going *anywhere*, do you understand me? I'm staying here with you."

• • •

Jasmine's first reaction was joy. A rush of happiness so strong, she could never harness it or make it manageable. It was a fist around her heart, pumping the blood without her assistance. Taking the responsibility of staying alive away from her. When a man like Sarge loved you with such ferocity, surely that love could sustain you on its own.

But she came down hard. She crashed to earth with broken bones, wondering why her parachute hadn't opened and softened the fall. *I've always,* always *loved you.*

How could she want that love and feel the unshakable need to run away at the same time? It was like walking in on the third act of a play and trying to discern each player's motivation, except there was only one player and his arms were banded around her so tight, she thought he might be trying to meld them together. A significant part of her wanted that joining to take place, but another more prominent part was scared to death. She'd allowed him to overwhelm her with every word, every touch. Now it was time to remove the blinders. And with that removal, every insecurity she'd slowly managed to suppress throughout the last few days rained down on her head.

Sarge couldn't want this woman she'd become, whose idea of a Friday night was warm beer in a shitty bar, fingernails still sooty from her factory job. This fantasy relationship would be over as soon as he realized he'd saddled himself with a never-was. Because Sarge Purcell, rock star, was the exact opposite. He'd made it.

It was up to Jasmine to make sure he didn't make this mistake. She…*she* would be the mistake. She couldn't compete with the bright lights and adoration he'd grown accustomed to since getting free of Hook.

Jasmine dug her fingernails into her palm, pressing until pain bloomed behind her eyes. "What do you mean you're staying?"

Sarge's head came up, wariness deepening the blue of his eyes at her tone of voice. God, he was beautiful, his dark hair a wreck, mouth red and shiny from kissing. "I mean I'm staying in Hook. I won't leave you. I can't."

His statements were little iron hooks digging into her organs. "Don't make promises in the heat of the moment. You're too good a person not to keep them."

"I don't even know what to say to that." A line formed between his eyebrows. "What about the part when I told you I love you, Jas? Let me know if you're planning on ignoring it, so I can say the words again. And again. Until you can't."

He wasn't going to make this easy. Had there been any doubt of that? Since he'd arrived, he'd come at her like a freight train, giving her no escape paths or places to burrow. "I heard you. I also heard you say *always*."

"That's right."

Jasmine expelled a quick breath, immediately wanting to draw it back into her lungs. She couldn't spare any oxygen when Sarge was sucking it all up. "You've been gone for four years. I'm not the same girl you think you love."

"Bullshit. You *are* that girl. Just like there's still some of the old Sarge still trapped inside me. We don't get away from our pasts, and if I've learned one damn thing, it's that we shouldn't always try. Not when they're the only thing that ever made you feel right."

"*No!*" The word emerged as a shout, laced with panic. Everything he said was designed to pull her under the surface, but she needed to kick for them both. Sarge was too young, too good, too *everything* to realize he was trying to doom himself. "I can't live up to the idea you have of me. I'm sorry, but you want something I can't give."

His hands slid down her arms and crashed onto the metal buffet. "Dammit, Jasmine. You're not giving either of us enough credit. You are that girl I loved. But you're also this *woman* I love, and I want her, too. This woman who doesn't blink at a bar fight. This woman whose voice got even more beautiful than the one I hear in my dreams. This woman I'm looking at right now. I *need* her."

Jasmine respected him all the more for making the point, but his astuteness did nothing to aid her cause. She couldn't allow his convenient logic to penetrate. There would be *other* logic later. *Different* points. But one truth wouldn't change — she didn't belong with him. "You should have told me from the beginning how you felt. This isn't fair." Sarge held fast when she tried to slide off the buffet. "You let me think this was casual, but it wasn't. Not for you."

"You're right." His thumb brushed over her knee. "You're right about that. I should have been honest. I can't find it in me to be sorry, though, Jasmine. Not when I know you *feel* something. Not when I know staying is the right thing."

*Staying. The right thing.* That's what it all came down to. Sarge's heart had always been on display, so apparent in everything he did. She would be no different. A responsibility he smiled through. People would laugh at their age difference, call him a fool for giving up the musician lifestyle to be with a woman seven years his senior. Eventually he would listen to the naysayers. No matter how well he hid his resentment, it would be there. Over turning down the contract, tossing away his chance at even greater success. God, it would kill her knowing she'd held him back. Forced him to squander his potential. The way she'd done.

"I'm sorry, I..." The words got lodged in her throat. He wouldn't listen to reason, so she had to be firm. Harsh. Already what came next haunted her, even with their bodies still joined. Swallowing the broken sound shivering up her throat, Jasmine wrestled with his grip until she could bypass Sarge, stooping down to pick up her jeans. "I'm sorry, I'm bowing out. I never would have let this happen if I thought you would want a relationship out of it."

When Jasmine straightened, Sarge was right behind her. "You don't think I see what you're doing?" He dragged her back against his chest, mouth pressed to her ear. "The man who loves you isn't afraid of a fight. Just tell me what I'm up against so I can knock it the fuck down."

It took a strength of will she'd never experienced to remain upright. To resist turning in Sarge's arms and confessing her doubts. Laying them on his doorstep and seeing what he could do with them. As if she didn't know. He would obliterate them somehow. For the moment. But they would grow back stronger and more insistent once time had a chance to pass. Once the outside world began to intrude. "Let me go."

"Never."

She pressed a hand to her mouth to stifle a sob, then pulled away with one remaining ounce of resolve. "I didn't mean for it to end like this. I would never intentionally hurt you…or River."

He stabbed the air with a finger. "We're the only two people involved here."

"That's not always how things work." When Jasmine finished pulling on her jeans and boots, it took her a minute to face Sarge. His face was grim, hands pushed into his pants pockets. Still as stone. Maybe she'd finally gotten through? Why did that possibility make her want to die? "I'll go out through the bar…there are probably a couple of cabs waiting by now. Do you mind going out the back?"

His laughter was sharp. "You sure know how to make a guy feel special."

Jasmine's face grew hot. "People shouldn't see us walking out of this room together. People's opinion of me is all I have. I have to *live* here, Sarge."

Two booted strides and Sarge was pushing into her personal space. "Maybe you didn't hear me the first time. I want to face them with you. I want to live here *with* you."

"Maybe you didn't hear me." She was fading, fading. It hurt to stand and talk and think. "That's n-not what I signed up for."

"Right." But she must have shown a dent in her armor, because a spark appeared in his eyes. A glimmer of the man she'd spent the day with, laughing and ignoring anything resembling the future. Sarge reached out and cupped her cheek and everything inside her went still. "I know it's a lot. I just told you I love you. That it's always been this way. Maybe you're even right to be scared, Jas, because this love is rough. It's sharp and sweet and dirty and jealous. It wakes me up in the middle of the night thinking I'm in the wrong place because you're not there. It believed you were mine before you saw me as a man, and the waiting...the *waiting* made this love bigger. It's so *big* and I understand why that's scary. I've had time to stop being scared of it, and you haven't." His hand slipped into Jasmine's hair, drawing her close so he could brush their mouths together. "I'll keep waiting. I'll wait out the fear."

She couldn't speak around the crushing sensation behind her ribs, so she simply shook her head, loosening tears that tracked down her cheeks.

The pull between them stole her breath, so intense there didn't seem any choice but to meet each other halfway. But Sarge tightened his grip on her hair and stepped back, pain evident in his handsome features. "Christmas Eve at the church. Will you be there?"

Two nights away. "Yes."

"Okay. I'll see you then." Attention locked on her, Sarge headed for the party room's back exit, pulling it open and pausing in the doorway. "At the very least, Jasmine, I just need to *see* you."

When the door clicked shut, Jasmine fell into the closest

folding chair. With the failure of her musical aspirations, getting stuck in a town she'd always imagined in her rear view, Jasmine had always thought of her life as a tragic series of disappointments. But as she sat in the still room listening to the rasp of her own breath, it became obvious she'd never understood tragedy until now. To have a man like Sarge and feel him waiting, feel him wanting, but not answer that call? It might very well stop her heart from beating.

At once, her bones ached. A tapping pain had started behind both eyes, forcing them shut. Home. If she didn't get home soon, she'd never find the willpower to move again. With a fortifying breath, Jasmine pushed to her feet, leaning down to fix her mussed hair in the reflective metal buffet. Wondering how in God's name she would talk to anyone and form complete sentences on the other side of the door, Jasmine nonetheless removed the metal chair poised beneath the knob and stepped out into the dim hallway.

Carmine leaned against the wall, tapping an empty beer bottle against his leg. It only took Jasmine half a second to deduce Carmine had been standing there a while. His lecherous grin said it all. Jasmine's stomach pitched, sending her stumbling forward a step. A yearning for Sarge hit her so fast and hard, a sob bubbled up from her throat. One wish. If she had one wish, Sarge would come thundering down the hallway to fold her up in his arms. But he wouldn't do that. He'd left. She'd sent him out through the back door like a dirty little secret.

"Saw you head in there with Purcell...he still in there?"

She didn't bother denying what Carmine had seen. "No."

His laugh was vulgar, making her feel even more exposed. "Seriously, Jasmine? I had no idea you liked your men so young. Guess my chances would have been shitty even if you didn't keep yourself locked up like a nun." He rubbed his whiskered chin. "Well. From *me*, anyway."

A burn started in her belly, spearing up to her throat. "Is that all you were waiting out here to tell me? Do you feel better now?"

"*God*." He kicked off the wall to face her. "Since day one, you've always thought you were so much better than us." When he gestured to the back room, the remains of his beer sloshed onto the floor. "Look what happens when you aim too high. The guy couldn't get out of here fast enough."

Even though it wasn't the truth, Jasmine's skin pulled tight. Just at the very idea of Sarge wanting to get away from her. Wasn't that her greatest fear when it came to being with him? "Are you finished?"

"How long do you think it would take before he found someone…younger?" Having reached his apparent point, Carmine's mouth tilted up on one end. "Probably won't even take him the walk home."

Jasmine waited for doubt to kick in. Waited for visions of Sarge touching someone else to play out like a grainy homemade movie in her head. But they didn't. Instead, she felt his mouth moving as it whispered promises against her ear. She saw him smiling at her across the car, both of them huffing into their hands to beat the chill. And underneath it all, there was bone-deep security. In *them*. Even if there couldn't be a *them*—a *them* would be selfish on her end—a *them* would be a united front against assholes like this. Carmine didn't know Sarge. He didn't know her, either. Not the Jasmine who straightened her spine and laughed.

Oh God, the laugh felt phenomenal. It twirled and waved pom-poms as she tried to move past Carmine in the hallway. When he stepped right to block her path, it reversed directions and cemented her hands into fists. "Back off."

"Last chance, Jasmine." He pinched a strand of her hair, rubbing it between his fingers. "You had your fun, now stop being unrealistic."

Carmine took one step closer, knocking her heels into the wall. In the space of a split second, a rebellion took place in her breast. Denial, anger, frustration welled and she embraced it. Embraced this part of her that had gone missing somewhere over the years. A gust of breath whooshed from her mouth, her closed fist lifting to sock Carmine in the jaw. She watched with openmouthed shock as he stumbled back with a wounded sound, hitting the opposite wall. But the shock turned to relief in a giant rush. There. There she was.

Jasmine heard a collective silence from the bar and turned, noticing the sea of attention they'd attracted. A week ago, she might have ducked and hightailed it out of the bar. Not tonight, though. Tonight, she calmly zipped her coat, smoothed back her hair and marched through the onlookers without so much as a blink. Just before the exit, a group of young women—the same ones who'd been taking pictures with Sarge—presented their palms for high fives, which she completed with a satisfying *slap*.

When the door closed behind her, she smiled. She smiled so wide it broke apart into a belly laugh as she climbed into the driver's seat of her car.

In that sweet, sparkling pocket of time, she wasn't a woman who could hold anyone back. Wasn't a woman who could cause anyone regret.

And she had some serious thinking to do.

# Chapter Fourteen

Sarge pulled open the double doors of his rented van, surveying the hundreds of packages that required unloading. To anyone else, carrying Christmas presents into the church event hall without help might resemble work. To him, it was pure saving grace. Distraction. One that would simultaneously prevent him from going to Jasmine's apartment and camping outside until she spoke to him, while doubling as a happy surprise for the kids of Hook. Hopefully. Buying a vanload of musical instruments had seemed like a great idea at the time, but now he kind of wondered if he should have gone with a sports theme.

Distracting thoughts were good.

They were also running short. Okay, they'd been running short for almost two days, since he'd left Jasmine at the Third Shift. He'd watched from across the street until she pulled away in her car, before taking a cab to Manhattan. An expensive drive, but a necessary one. Jasmine needed time to process the love-bomb he'd detonated. If he waited around in Hook, nothing short of imprisonment would have kept him from trying to dig out the shrapnel he'd sent flying. So he'd spent two days on the phone with a Realtor, looking for a place to buy in Hook. Then he'd gone shopping for child-friendly instruments. And drinking. He'd done some drinking. The way a man did when his happiness hung in the balance.

Already his back muscles were tense, his palms damp, just knowing he would see Jasmine soon. Not kissing the crap out of her on sight was going to be some serious bullshit. It might actually kill him resisting that mouth now. *Now* was not like *before*. Before, he'd had fantasies. Now he had truth. And the truth was, her mouth spoke words he needed to hear. Gave pleasure he needed to receive. Could deny or approve the future he craved with his goddamn soul.

"So let's unload some fucking ukuleles, huh?" Sarge muttered, planting a fist against the van's metal door with a loud *whap*.

"Sounds like a party," came a familiar female voice behind him.

Sarge turned to find Lita perched on the hood of James's Mustang, threading neon-green shoelaces through the holes of a boot, leaving one of her feet bare. Already knowing he'd find his manager in the driver's seat—where Lita went, so followed James—Sarge sent him a wave without looking. "What are you doing here?"

"Heard you lined up a gig tonight."

"Where'd you hear that?"

"TMZ."

"Jesus." Sarge dragged a hand down his face. "I'm just playing a couple Christmas songs. Doesn't really qualify as a gig."

Lita shoved her foot into the freshly laced boot. "We're a band, Sergeant. It's kind of a package deal."

Too exhausted to give the drummer a hard time about the nickname, Sarge unloaded a crate of maracas. "If we're a package deal, where's our bass player?"

"Asleep in the backseat."

"Right." He stacked two more crates of jingling instruments on top of the maracas and strode toward the church hall, where a group of administrators waited to direct him. Halfway there, Sarge stopped and turned with a curse. Being a prick to his band wasn't going to solve his immediate problem. Convenient or not, they'd come to support him. They weren't responsible for the heartbeat pumping out of tune inside his chest. Sarge caught Lita's eye, tipping his head toward the administrators. "Just tell them you're with the band."

Lita's expression went from wary to relieved. "I bet they weren't expecting a Spice Girls reunion." She rapped on the windshield. "Look alive, James. We've got a gig in a motherfucking church."

Sarge carried the crates into the hall, shaking his head as he went. When Lita, James, and their groggy bass player helped with the unloading, he was surprised at first, until he noticed the concerned glances in his direction. On a trip to the van, Sarge caught up with James. "You told them I was staying with Jasmine, didn't you?"

James adjusted his sunglasses. "I don't participate in gossip."

Okay. That was accurate. None of them did. Still... "Lita just gave me the awkward shoulder pat of the century. Something's up."

As if the sky would fall down if he were forced to converse, James dropped his head forward on a sigh. "There's a video of you and Jasmine in a toy store...it's circulating."

A throb pushed at his jugular. "When you say circulating..."

"A few million hits."

"Oh. Great." He ripped a hand through his hair. "That

might account for why I haven't heard from her."

"I sent you the video days ago. You should check your email."

"Email," Sarge repeated for no reason, his voice dull.

Lita pushed between the two men on her way to the van. "Hey, what if I played an entire set on one of these mini drum sets? We could all pretend like it was completely normal and everyone would trip balls."

James's lips twitched.

Sarge started to question them both about their motives for coming to New Jersey, when Lita slammed the van door and crossed her arms, staring at something past Sarge's shoulder. "Don't look now, but Yoko just showed up."

"Yoko?" Sarge turned—and almost staggered back with the impact of seeing Jasmine when he hadn't been expecting it. Or had time to brace himself. She was dressed up for Christmas Eve, dark hair piled on top of her head, lips painted the color of cranberries. Her legs looked an extra mile long, thanks to a pair of black high heels that Sarge instantly wanted to hear hit the floor. She stopped short upon seeing them, pulling her winter coat tighter around her body.

*Dammit, I should be the one warming her up.*

The fact that she remained between the rows of cars, as if someone had hit a pause button, made him want to rage at the darkening sky. She should have walked faster or beckoned him closer. Not stopped. *Never* stopped. Did that mean she was sticking to her decision? Fuck. That.

"Can you two head inside?"

James indicated the church in a "ladies first" gesture for Lita, but the drummer took her time sauntering past, giving Jasmine a lazy once-over. "I saw the video. You've got pipes, I'll give you that."

"*Lita…*" Sarge warned.

"I'm just *saying*." The drummer held up both hands. "If

she wants to sing with the band, she should come around for a legit tryout. This is a democracy."

Gratefulness flooded Sarge, so much that he was actually able to nod at Lita in the face of Jasmine rejecting him. Not an easy feat. A minute later, James had shuffled Sarge's bandmate off to the church, leaving him standing alone with Jasmine. Not really alone, though, since the parking lot was filling around them. Parents wrapped scarves around their children and guided them inside; Hook residents called "merry Christmas" to one another over the hum of car engines; the cold wind picked up around all of it, making the church parking lot feel like the inside of a snow globe. One that needed to be shaken until it put Jasmine in his arms.

"Merry Christmas, Jas."

She adjusted the pink bakery box on her hip, making him notice it for the first time. "Merry Christmas, Sarge."

He'd been right. This was indeed some serious bullshit. Conscious of the multitude of people with them in the parking lot, Sarge closed the distance between him and Jasmine, angling his body so no one would see his face. "What's in the box?"

"Um." She looked down, obviously thrown by the question. "Cheesecake."

"Huh." He tilted his head. "Fruit topping?"

She shifted in her heels. "Strawberries. Why are you asking me this?"

"Not sure. I think I'm kind of enjoying how impossible small talk is between us." He took one more step closer, bringing them less than a foot apart. God, what he wouldn't have given to knock the box out of her hand and shove her up against a parked car. It wouldn't take much to get that dress up around her waist, would it? Somehow, though, he maintained the scant distance separating them. "Nice weather we're having, right?"

"Stop it."

Sarge leaned back, allowing his gaze to travel up her stocking-clad legs, over the curve of her hip. "I think we'll have snow for Christmas."

A white cloud of air puffed from her cranberry lips. "I'm going inside."

Jasmine took one step to bypass him, and just a simple brush of their shoulders seemed to break them both. She made a small sound, heels scuffing on the concrete. Sarge snagged an arm around her waist and dragged her back around, into the warmth of his body. Right where they fit. Right where she belonged. The pastry box plonked onto the ground, but neither one of them moved to pick it up as Sarge walked them back, using a van to hide them from view.

"You're so angry."

Hardball pitches, one by one, landed in his midsection, hearing those whispered words. But denying the accusation in them would be a lie. "Of course I'm angry. You looked nervous to see me. You know how much I hate that?"

"Not nervous." She wet her lips. "Okay, maybe a little nervous."

His forehead dropped to rest on hers. "Baby, you want my mouth."

It hadn't been posed as a question, but it was still for her to answer. "I don't…know if that's wise. I haven't—"

"Changed your mind. I know." Or he did now, anyway. Sarge ignored the drilling pain and focused on her eyes. She shook her head and started to speak again, but he pressed a thumb to her lips. "We can go back to bullshit and small talk afterward. I'll just need your taste on my tongue to get through it."

Her eyelids fell. "We can't keep doing this." She struggled a little in his grip. "After what you told me, I have no excuse. I would be leading you on."

"Lead me on, then." He lifted her off the ground, planting her backside against the nearest car trunk and fusing their bodies together. "I'm asking you to lead me on. There's your permission. Make me believe this is real."

"You can't ask me to do that—"

Sarge kissed the words off her mouth. He could almost feel them crumbling under the impact of his lips and tongue. The occasional raking of his teeth over her full lower lip. Wind whistled past, but couldn't drown out their mutual heartbeats. His galloped like a runaway horse in his ears...and Jasmine's. He could hear it, would hear it a country away, wouldn't he? It sounded like he'd heard it eight thousand times, when logic told him that was impossible. Her body shifted between him and the car trunk, her hands tugging him closer...then pushing him away. Away. Away?

"*Sarge.*"

He'd been expecting Jasmine's voice, but it was Adeline, calling him from the church entrance. He and Jasmine traded breaths for a heavy moment before he turned his head and called, "Yeah?"

A low chuckle. "Your band is ready, but they have no lead singer. Know anyone who could help them out?"

"Be there in a minute." He returned his attention to Jasmine.

"Go," she whispered.

He hated that word coming from the swollen mouth he'd just kissed. "I smeared your lipstick."

"I know." Her tits were lifting and falling so fast. Up and down. Dragging over his chest. "It's all over your mouth."

Sarge couldn't resist. "Wipe it off."

She looked to be considering it, but shook her head. "No."

"Wipe it off or I'll be wearing it on stage."

"Jesus." Jasmine actually laughed, and it calmed some of the thunderheads clashing in his brain. Using her thumb, she wiped away the cranberry coloring, pulling away quickly when his tongue licked out to taste her. "You're good to go."

Cursing church people for being so damn punctual, Sarge backed away. "I'll find you afterward."

She didn't say anything for a long beat. "I don't doubt it."

There was something unusual in the way she said it, but Adeline shouted his name again, giving Sarge no choice but to solve the puzzle of Jasmine later.

• • •

If Sarge would've given Jasmine a minute to speak, she would have told him.

She wouldn't be letting him go.

Since that night in the Third Shift when she'd stood up to Carmine and felt the transformation in herself, Jasmine had given herself one long, continuous wake-up slap in the face. Sarge was a man with the ability to decide his own life path. He'd determined that path would be walked with her. It meant staying in Hook. It meant she had to trust him to know what he needed.

It also meant she needed to trust her own gut. Needed to listen to her mind and heart when they sang in perfect harmony for one man. There would be people, like Carmine, who took bets on how long their relationship would last. There would be laughing behind their backs—probably even a lot of uttering of a certain word that started with *c* and ended with *ougar*. But none of it would register when she and Sarge were together. Alone or in public, the outside world only ever seemed like a minor detail. What mattered was them. How they made each other feel.

And God, he made her feel *so much*.

It hadn't felt right kissing him in the parking lot. Not when he thought she'd let him go without a fight. God, he'd already looked haunted, his kisses feeling so final. Tonight. She would tell him tonight. When they weren't in a freezing parking lot, being peeped on by passersby in the parking lot.

Jasmine eased out of her coat and took a spot at the rear of the hall, just in time for Old News to walk on stage. A low thrumming started in her belly at seeing Sarge in his official front man capacity. Already he was a sexy, charismatic package, but it was amplified when he picked up his guitar. He played a few strings, winking at the crowd when they howled in response. Then he found her through the crowd and made a growling sound into the microphone.

*Dios.* As soon as this party ended, she was taking him home and rocking his ever-loving world. The neighbors might even call the police.

*Let them.*

"Okay, this first song is for my niece, Marcy, the coolest kid in Hook." He smiled down at the front row, where all the children, including Marcy, were lined up. "Did you guys know she taught me how to play the guitar?"

A chorus of laughter went up, from the children and parents alike. Several mothers relaxed a little when it became obvious Sarge and Old News would be making the show kid-friendly. Jasmine's smile widened when he launched into an acoustic version of "Frosty the Snowman," signaling to his bandmates to come in on the second verse, since clearly the band hadn't rehearsed. Somehow that made it even more special. When a man leaned against the wall beside Jasmine, she recognized him from being in the parking lot with Sarge. He was tall, with a slight dusting of salt and pepper at his temples and stress lines around his eyes, but he couldn't have been older than thirty-five. Handsome in a hard, distinguished way. Against a backdrop of ill-fitting Christmas sweaters, his polished appearance stood out, making him look more suitable for a polo match than a casual church function.

"Merry Christmas," Jasmine murmured, unable to stop herself from facing the stage, where Sarge was now using his fingers to mimic antlers. "How do you know Sarge?"

The man followed her line of vision and dipped his chin. "I manage Old News. Although I'm not sure who's managing who anymore." He extended a hand. "I'm James Brandon. Nice to meet you."

Jasmine shook James's hand, seeing him in a new light. This man had spent years on the road with Sarge, probably making a boatload of cash in the process. How would he feel when Sarge decided to stay in Hook? "Nice to meet you, too."

They were quiet for a time, but there was an air of discomfort between them. She could feel James building up to something and started to excuse herself, somehow knowing she wouldn't want to know, but he beat her to the punch. "Look. Jasmine." He straightened his collar. "I'm going to be blunt with you. If tonight turned out to be the final time Old News played together, I wouldn't try to talk them out of it. I could walk away." A glance toward the stage, specifically the drummer. "From most of it."

"Why are you telling me this?"

James appeared to be choosing his words. "It was impossible to live with Sarge and not be aware of his feelings for you. He wears them like clothes. They're in every song, in the background noise of every interview." The manager nodded toward the stage. "He'd give it all up in a heartbeat for you. And if it were me…before I let him do that, I would want to know exactly what giving it up means."

Her lips felt numb, but she forced the words out, already knowing nothing would be the same when James finished speaking. "Tell me."

"The new contract would mean another full album by summer. A world tour to promote it." The manager looked like he'd swallowed something made of spikes. "We've been traveling on a bus until now, but the new contract would mean private jets. No more questionable motels or small venues. It's the next level. And since we're free agents at the moment, so to speak, they've quadrupled their offer to make us sign."

If the ground cracked in half and sucked her in just then, Jasmine would have gone happily. A host of emotions fought for precedence inside her. Disgust at herself for considering asking Sarge to remain in Hook, thus relinquishing the multitude of opportunities yet to come. Gratefulness to James for being honest with her, because Jasmine knew—without a *doubt*—Sarge never would have told her the facts. Lastly, she felt a freezing shower of sorrow and loss, soaking her down to the skin. "I can't let him pass that up," she managed. "The whole band would lose out, too."

"If I may make a suggestion?" When she nodded, James swiped a hand down his jaw. "Just make him a part of the decision. Don't cut him out."

Jasmine watched the manager stride away with a mixture of dread and shock. *Don't cut him out.* But what choice did she have? She'd let her newfound confidence make her selfish, let it blind her to what would matter to Sarge. Oh God, it would kill her to let him leave, especially after deciding to give their relationship a chance, but it was the right thing. She'd gotten stuck in Hook, but no way in hell would she be the reason for Sarge doing the same. It had to end. It had to be tonight, before she gave him any false hope.

Sarge had brought some children up on stage to dance, but his gaze cut to hers swiftly, making Jasmine wonder if she'd called his name out loud. Her sinking heart must have been obvious, because his indulgent smile slipped in response. Unable to stand being this close to him and knowing what was to come, Jasmine wove through the crowd and beelined for the ladies' room.

. . .

After seeing—*feeling*—the light go out of Jasmine's eyes from across the room, their set could not have ended fast enough for Sarge. Something was wrong. He needed to find her. Now. Needed to figure out how to fix it. In the parking lot before the show, there hadn't been a sense of loss jackhammering him in the neck. There hadn't been a driving urgency to get Jasmine in a corner and demand to know every thought in her head. Right now, it was all he could think about.

Unfortunately, about forty people were lined up to take photos with him and shake his hand. Lita and James were speaking in hushed tones behind the makeshift stage, leaving him to work the crowd alone. Any attempts to escape were thwarted, though, as he received unnecessary gratitude for putting on the show, for bringing presents for the children. He mumbled his way through it, scribbling his signature on everything from baseball caps to church programs. When he finally managed to break free, he strode for the back hallway where he'd seen Jasmine disappear during their third song, but his progress ground to a halt when his sister, River, snagged his attention.

River looked…distressed. In a way he'd never seen her. And when she directed it straight at him, Sarge knew exactly what it was about. It only took a few seconds for them to meet halfway in a quiet corner of the hall, but it took her twice as long to start speaking. It alarmed him, the way she couldn't seem to draw a decent breath. "Riv—"

"How could you do that, Sarge?" She covered her mouth with a cupped palm. "You shouldn't have. I-I don't know what I'm going to do now."

River pulled away when Sarge tried to lay a hand on her arm, so he stepped closer and lowered his voice. "What happened?"

"Vaughn. He left me a voicemail. At the church with Adeline, since he doesn't have my home number anymore." She paused, as if replaying the message in her head. "It was short, but he said you overnighted him a letter."

God, had it only been a couple days since he'd sent that letter? It felt like a month had passed. "When things ended between you and Vaughn… River, he didn't even *know* you were pregnant."

"It didn't matter. I *still* doesn't. Do you think I want to be with someone who doesn't want me?" River's gaze found Marcy across the room where she stood, watching the big kids test out tambourines. "I was going to do right by Marcy with or without Vaughn—and I have. I've done the best I can."

Sarge grasped her shoulders. "You've done unbelievable, Riv. Marcy is just…she's everything." He dipped down so their eyes were level. "But we've known Vaughn a long time. Or we used to. The guy I remember would want to know you were struggling. He would be sick knowing you were doing this all alone."

"I'm *not* alone," she said, visibly upset by his words. "I have friends. Good people around me who love my daughter and help when they can."

It hurt when River didn't mention him, but he camouflaged it. "The money I send you goes straight into a college fund. You don't even use it." He blew out a frustrated breath. "You shouldn't have to work two jobs. You shouldn't be so exhausted."

She twisted away on an uncharacteristic curse, then came back. "Who told you all this? About the night job?"

"Adeline. Who else?"

His attempt at levity died a quick death, River still looking shaken. "You didn't see him when he came back from overseas. He's not the same person he was in high school." She hiccuped into her wrist. "And now he's on his way to Hook."

"What?" Sarge shook his head, pressure weighing down on him, pushing him toward the floor. "No, I asked him to… call you. Or write back. It wasn't supposed to happen this fast."

The fight went out of River, and that wounded Sarge more than anything. "You know, there was a little part of me that imagined Vaughn running back once he knew. Wanting to be a father for Marcy." She stared at something invisible over his shoulder. "But it's too late for that. Way too late. Worse…that might not even be what he wants. That's what will hurt the worst."

"I'm sorry." Sarge pulled his sister into a hug, but her arms remained slack at her sides. "I didn't think it through, River. I thought I was helping." When River didn't respond, he tightened his hold. "But I'll be here now to help. I'm not going anywhere. You don't want to use the money, fine. You'll have me. I'll get the hang of babysitting."

River pulled away. "What are you saying?"

He gestured toward the packed church hall. "I'm staying in Hook."

"For me and Marcy?"

"Well, yeah." That would be enough reason. His sister needed his help, and he'd been absent too long. He hoped with every fiber of his being he would be staying for Jasmine, too. But he didn't know yet. She hadn't decided if she wanted anything permanent with him. Fuck, that uncertainty opened a fresh pothole in his sternum. "Yeah, Riv. I want to be here for you guys."

"*No.*" Based on his sister's expression, she'd surprised them both with the denial. "No. I want to do this on my own, Sarge. I *need* to, okay? I was reliant on our parents, then Vaughn…and when they left for Florida, all I had was *me*. And I was weak. But I'm not weak now. That's why I don't use your money, because I'm proving myself. I'm proud of what

I've managed to accomplish alone." She swiped at a tear on her cheek. "So…no. I don't want you moving here to save me. I'm saving myself."

The pothole in his chest deepened. "Riv, I—"

"I'm sorry. I don't mean to hurt you." She squeezed his forearm. "I really hope you'll come visit. But you need to get back out there and make us proud, okay? Show Marcy what can happen if she dreams big."

Maybe Sarge should've taken his sister's rejection in the spirit it was intended. River didn't have a mean bone in her body, and on some level, he understood why she needed to prove herself. Of course he did. But in the wake of Jasmine pushing him away, all he heard was another person he loved saying…*leave*. They didn't need or want him. His staying in Hook wasn't a positive, but a negative. A burden. God, weren't they kind of right? He'd waltzed into town like a hero trying to solve River's problems, deceiving Jasmine by proposing a purely physical relationship, when in actuality, he'd been in love with her from the start. Jesus. Maybe they were right.

Maybe he should do everyone a favor and get gone.

Jasmine chose that moment to fill his vision, so goddamn pretty in her red dress and stockings, it choked him up. And that was *before* he saw her expression. Once he took in her sympathy and distress, swallowing became impossible. She really didn't even need to say a word for him to catch the drift. Over. They were over. She didn't want him hanging around, same as his family.

"Sarge, can we talk now?"

His laughter was jagged. "Listen, Jas. I'm just going to save you the trouble, all right? I'll leave. I'm out." Her confused frown baffled him. Shouldn't she look relieved? Dammit, he didn't have the right to feel angry. This fantasy scenario of being part of his family again, settling down with the girl of his dreams? That's all it was. A fantasy fabricated in his head, while everyone built lives without him. He had no right being mad they wanted to keep what they'd built. But he *was* mad. His gut felt torn down the middle with it. "Is there something else you're waiting for me to say? Is there something I haven't said over and fucking over since I got here? There's nothing left but good-bye, right?"

Ah shit, just saying good-bye while looking at Jasmine was eating him alive. He had to get out of there now. Before he did something insane, like press his face against her legs and ask what else he could have done. Yeah…yeah, he had to walk toward the door, get in his van, and find a place to hole up. Couldn't let everything rush in on him right now, or Jasmine would only feel guiltier than she already looked. He hated that guilt. Wanted to kiss it off her face, but would never get that chance again.

Something hard and leather pressed against Sarge's palm, and he looked down to find his guitar case, Lita in his periphery. For the second time that night, he was grateful to the drummer. Holding his guitar proved to be the push he needed to give Jasmine one final memorizing look before exiting into the dark chill of night.

# Chapter Fifteen

As far as Christmas mornings went, this one was somber as hell.

Following tradition, Jasmine had shown up at River's house to watch Marcy open presents before spending the rest of the holiday with her parents. She hadn't had a chance to speak with her best friend since Sarge's departure last night, but it was obvious they were both making a Herculean effort to stay positive for Marcy's sake. Currently, the three-year-old was tearing through wrapping paper with glee as River followed with a black trash bag.

Jasmine felt like she'd been covered in cement. Her movements felt sluggish, and no number of commands sent to her brain could hasten them. She'd managed to wait five full minutes after Sarge blew out of the church hall before leaving herself—and it had been a rapid downhill shot from there. Her eyes felt like they'd been rubbed raw with sand she'd cried so much. Huge, racking sobs that reminded her of a devastated child, which wasn't so far off. Years seemed to have been stripped away, leaving her bare, with no experience to pull from.

How did she go about getting over this? How did anyone? If she ever found the wherewithal to speak to anyone about the loss that was caving in her stomach, what would they say? Probably that it would get easier in degrees. Well, the next degree over from her current state was still bereft. So was the degree after that. And the one beside that. So Jasmine was pretty sure she'd be living inside this swamp of pummeling pain a good, long while.

River handed her a cup of eggnog with nutmeg sprinkled on top, but she only stared down into it without drinking. "Thanks."

"Are you all right?" River asked.

"Are you?"

They stared at each other until Marcy bounced over, flushed from excitement. "Who are these ones from, Mom?" She handed two silver-wrapped presents to River and brushed her loose curls back. "Can I open it?"

River checked the tag. "They're from Uncle Sarge...they were delivered yesterday. One for you and one for me." She turned the packages over in her hands. "And these are extra presents, Marcy. Uncle Sarge already bought you the guitar."

Marcy whooped. "Thank you, Uncle Sarge."

A line formed between River's brows, reminding Jasmine so much of Sarge she felt pricks behind her eyelids. With more eagerness than she had the right to feel, Jasmine watched mother and daughter open the packages from Sarge, watched them smile at what they found. Matching bomber jackets with the Old News logo on the back, their names stitched over the pocket. River stared down at hers while Marcy worked her arms into the sleeves. "We'll have to send him a thank-you card when he gets back to L.A. If he's not already there."

Needing to move, Jasmine stood and walked to the closest window, looking out over the side yard. He could be an entire country away at that very moment. All she'd had to do was throw her arms around him instead of making him leave. It would have been so easy. But there had been a reason for her decision. She needed to remember that. Even if in the light of day, nothing seemed a good enough excuse for his absence. Even if the business card James had slipped into her hand on his way out burned in her pocket, tempting her to find out at least where he'd gone.

"Jasmine, there's one for you, too."

She turned to find River holding out a silver box. Perhaps it was the worst idea possible, but she grabbed on to the gift like a lifeline. Something—anything—that would remind her of Sarge. Conscious of River watching, Jasmine ran her index finger beneath the folded edge so as not to rip it. She slid the medium-sized box out of one end and tipped the lid back. Inside white tissue paper was a bomber jacket, just like the ones he'd sent River and Marcy.

Except when she turned her jacket over, it didn't say Old News on the back. Bright neon-green beading spelled out the name Bon Jovi. A cross between a laugh and a sob broke free of her mouth as she picked up the card and opened it.

*Never get into an ugly clothing war with a Jersey man, when bragging rights are on the line. I love you, Sarge.*

"Oh God." Jasmine dropped the box along with the jacket, pressing both hands over her heart. "I can't do this."

River stooped down to pick up the jacket, watching Jasmine with concern as she went. "You can't do what?"

"Pretend everything is fine. Like he didn't come here and make me"—Jasmine's eyelids fluttered shut, the organ pounding beneath her palms with increased force—"make me fall in love with him."

"Oh, Jas…"

She took back the jacket from River, running her fingers over the collar. "How am I supposed to go back to being without him? Nothing feels or looks or sounds the same." At once, her breathing grew labored, like she'd sprinted a mile. "I miss him. And I know its wrong and selfish to want him, but I do. It doesn't even have to be here. Just anywhere."

When the silence stretched, Jasmine lifted her head to find River giving her a sad, sweet smile. "There's your answer."

"I don't understand."

River picked up Marcy and settled the little girl on her hip. "You said you want to be with him anywhere." She shrugged one shoulder. "It doesn't have to be Hook. Go find him, Jas. And then go *with* him."

A hysterical laugh bubbled from her throat. "I can't leave here." She'd stopped believing she ever could. Shoved those hopes and dreams way too deep to unearth them ever again. Hadn't she? "My job…my family. You and Marcy. Everything is here."

"Yeah. We're not going anywhere, either." River tugged on the hem of Jasmine's shirt. "We'll talk all the time. You'll come for visits. Maybe someday you'll want to come back and settle. And we'll pick up right where we're leaving off."

Jasmine could barely see through her tears. "You sound so sure."

River kissed her daughter's head. "Jasmine, are you sure about Sarge?"

"*Yes*," she whispered.

"That's all I need to hear. *Go*."

• • •

Sarge sat on the floor of his hotel room, back pressed against the bed. His oversize headphones hugged his ears, delivering Morrissey at top volume. Crumpled notebook paper was strewn over every inch of the floor, mocking him. Little balls of failure. Around his sixty-third attempt to write a song about Jasmine, Sarge thought he was onto something. He'd titled it "Gold." That single word was the only accurate way to describe how she smelled, but he couldn't get the feeling to translate onto paper. It was all garbage compared to the real thing. *All* his songs were now. He'd written them *before*. And he was living in an *after* world.

There was a tray of room service food on the desk across the room, but he had no recollection of how it came to be there. Or when it appeared. The smell of grease was making him sick, though. Sick on top of sick on top of sick. God, why didn't the fucking volume go any higher on his headphones? He couldn't drown out the...*gold*. Jasmine's tongue sliding along his belly. Holding her hand in the mall. That unrestrained laugh she'd let loose when he tickled her.

Sarge shot forward to his knees and snagged the almost-empty notebook off the floor, whipping the pen from his pocket.

*Golden laughter. Never after—*

Garbage.

He tore the piece of paper in half with a satisfying rip, crumpling both sides and throwing them in opposite directions. Songwriting had always been his way of coping with the solitude. Being in a sea of thousands but feeling completely alone. It wasn't working now. Nothing compared to the days he'd spent in Hook with Jasmine. They'd written the perfect song just by being together, and he would never come close to matching it.

The curtains of his hotel room were drawn, casting the room in darkness except for one dim lamp in the corner. At some point he'd even found that minimal light offensive and covered it with his T-shirt, leaving him unclothed save a pair of black sweatpants. Outside he could hear bells ringing for donations. Could hear snowplows scraping down the city streets of Manhattan, clearing away the snow that continued to fall. Christmas Day. He wanted nothing to do with it. Wanted nothing to do with the new recording deal. Another few years on the road, knowing where he *really* wanted to be was with a woman he couldn't have?

*I don't have it in me. I have nothing left in me.*

It was unclear when or how he would leave this hotel room. Eventually he would either be thrown out or walk through the exit of his own accord. But it wouldn't be happening today. Or tomorrow. Not until he wrote a fucking song to adequately describe the woman he was in love with. At least then he would have something to show for the misery.

Sarge shoved back his unbrushed hair, scrubbing at his bleary eyes until the notebook once again came into focus. His pen had just touched paper when light appeared to his left. Someone else bringing him french fries or wanting to clean the room. They were probably speaking to him, but answering would require him to remove the noise over his ears, and then thoughts would rush in. *No thank you.* He was just about capable of fielding the sneaky memories trickling in through the deafening lyrics.

When warm skin brushed against Sarge's face, he recoiled, as though a bullet had struck him in the chest. It forced him to suck in air. And with that air came gold. Jasmine's gold. She was there. Standing in the hotel room, framed by the still-open door. Sarge glanced behind Jasmine long enough to determine she'd been let in by James before consuming the sight of her again. So goddamn beautiful. But the door closed, and she went too dark. No. *No, no, no.* Sarge lunged to his feet, feeling along the wall for a decent source of light. *There.* He found a standing floor lamp and turned it on, illuminating Jasmine where she stood at the foot of his bed.

Morrissey was still singing in his ears about heaven knowing he was miserable, and it seemed like a huge risk, removing the headphones. What if she was there to apologize for hurting him, but wanted to explain her standpoint? Or some other possibility that didn't end in them together? And why—*why*—couldn't they just *be* together when his heart was clearly being operated from the palm of her hand? If she rejected him again, right in the center of this agony, he wouldn't have the strength to come back.

When he didn't immediately remove his headphones, Jasmine nodded, as if she completely understood the nonsensical fuckery happening in his sleep-deprived brain. Instead of trying to talk to him through the noise, though, she knelt down on the ground and picked up one of his discarded pieces of paper. She read it, her gorgeous lips moving, before lifting wet eyes to him. The sight of her kneeling, her expression pleading, knocked the remaining breath from his lungs.

"Love you, love you…" Sarge murmured, unaware if the words came out the way they sounded in his head. Jasmine ducked her head in response, then set about picking up every balled-up sheet on the floor, reading them, and stacking them in a pile. Sarge watched her, afraid to move, knowing the words were unworthy of her but unable to resist seeing her acknowledgment of them. *Look at them. Look. See how I feel? See what you did?*

Finally, she was finished clearing the room of trashed lyrics. Nothing left. The Morrissey album had finished, leaving Sarge with only the echo of his deep, shaking inhales. The far-off sounds of Jasmine moving across the floor on her knees to pick up the notebook he'd left lying open. She picked up the pen and started to write, hair falling on the floor as she leaned forward. Somehow he knew the vision of Jasmine biting her lip and moving the pen inside his notebook would be the last thing he thought about before he died. Just knew it, right then and there.

Something like five minutes or five hours had passed

when she stood up, hesitating a few beats before handing him the book. Sarge could barely rip his gaze from her to read what she'd written, but managed it through sheer force of will.

> *Got turned around when you crashed through*
> *Couldn't stay away from you.*
> *Swept me up and shook me down.*
> *Blindsided. Sunk. Lost you, too.*
>
> *Forgot how to leap when I looked at you.*
> *But I see clear now. You made me new.*
> *Take me. Keep me. Love me back.*
> *Can I still be your girl in blue?*

The notebook slipped free of Sarge's fingers, falling in a flutter of white to the ground. When it didn't make a sound, he realized the headphones were still covering his ears and tore them off, flinging them to the side. Unable to regulate the pounding of his heart or rasping of his breath, Sarge framed Jasmine's face in his hands.

"Love you back, Jasmine?" He searched her face. "Love you *back*?"

Tears decorated her cheeks as she nodded, but Sarge only had a moment to savor the confirmation that she actually... *loved* him back, before Jasmine buried her face in his chest. "I'm sorry," came her muffled voice. "I could feel it when you left Hook. Could feel that you were gone. And nothing felt right anymore."

Sarge's feet weren't even on solid ground yet after hearing that Jasmine loved him. He definitely wasn't in any shape to hear things like *that*, much less process them. "Jesus. Just... give me a minute or you're going to kill me."

"What?" She pulled back to swipe at her eyes. "I-I just need you to know. Being without you, even for a day...it hurt so bad—"

His mouth stamped over hers with a growl, sealing off her words. He stayed that way, keeping their mouths meshed together—not allowing himself to use his tongue— until he could think somewhat straight. Cautiously, he eased back an inch. "You love me and you hurt without me? Okay. Thank God." Sarge heaved in a breath. "But that's all I can handle for one day. My heart went from empty to full too fast."

Jasmine ran her fingertips up his sides. "But there are more words inside me."

Inside Sarge's chest, that pounding organ seized so tight, he had to swallow a gasp. "Save them for tomorrow. And the day after that." Walking her backward toward the bed, he kissed her with building fervor. "And the day after that. We have time now. We have *time*, baby."

"Every day," Jasmine whispered, just before her back hit the mattress. "I'll tell you more every day."

Sarge licked a path over Jasmine's cleavage as he shoved down his sweatpants with one hand. "Fuck it. Tell me now."

Jasmine locked her legs around his waist and arched her back. "I love your voice, how it goes a little rough when you say my name. I love the calluses on your hands. I love you for singing 'Frosty the Snowman'—"

"Enough. I can't." Sarge pinned their foreheads together. "Merry Christmas, Jas. God. *God*, I love you." He heaved a breath against her mouth. "I have for such a long time."

She kissed him hard. "Catching up is going to be half the fun."

# Epilogue

"Why did you wear pants?" Sarge groaned into the back of Jasmine's head. "Why would you *ever* wear pants?"

Her smug answering smile was fleeting because Sarge went to work on her neck, running his teeth over the spot he'd discovered at the slope of her shoulder. Warm, wet, sexual kisses that weakened her knees as Sarge's day-old beard abraded her skin. Totally her fault since she hadn't given him time to shave before leaving the house. They were backstage in Sarge's dressing room, five minutes from showtime, and—

Yup. His hand had definitely snaked around her hip to unbutton the jeans she'd chosen to wear, *just* to avoid a late arrival for Sarge on stage. Since arriving in Los Angeles to begin work on the newly contracted album, she'd been culpable for Sarge's lateness to three press events, five recording sessions, and one charity event, which both of them still felt guilty about. Jasmine liked to think back to Sarge's promise that his relative youth would mean needing her more often. And then she liked to laugh over his underestimation. Before the limousine had picked them up to transport them to the show, he'd taken her up against the living room wall, one of her legs still stuck in the jeans she wore now. Her boyfriend was insatiable. And she didn't have a single damn complaint.

"Ahhh," Jasmine breathed when Sarge pushed his erection against her bottom, bringing her up against the waist-high dressing table. "We can't."

"We already *would* have if you'd worn a skirt." He tangled a hand in her hair, turning her head to the side for a slippery, over-the-shoulder kiss. "This is why I made the no-pants rule at the house. All panties, all the time."

"Rules were made to be broken."

Jasmine's words ended on a squeal of laughter when Sarge whirled her around, boosting her up onto the table and easing between her legs. For a minute, they just looked at each other, breath mingling between them. Moments like this weren't unusual since they'd taken that cross-country flight and landed in Los Angeles. Their first week had been spent in a hotel while house hunting. At first, Jasmine had been a little alarmed by the prices of the houses Sarge wanted for them. Coastline property in Malibu wasn't exactly in her range, even though she'd been saving money since she'd started at the factory and insisted on contributing what she could. But true to character, Sarge had been adamant about giving her the best, so in the end she'd relented, allowing him to put both of their names on the deed to an oceanfront home overlooking the Pacific. Jasmine's one condition had been her helping to pay for household costs and maintenance, which meant she'd had to work fast to find a job. Which she had.

Jasmine now taught voice lessons in downtown Los Angeles. And her heart had never been so full. Doing what she loved during the day and returning to the man she loved at night. Her client roster was brimming with talent, due in

part to the viral video of her singing in a certain toy store…
and one super-famous boyfriend who tended to make surprise
drop-ins during lessons. Life was damn good.

"You going to come out and sing with me tonight?"
Sarge whispered, nipping at her lower lip. "James says they're
demanding you on Twitter and the message boards." He
tucked a strand of hair behind her ear. "We can sing that new
song we've been working on."

Her boyfriend's sweet torture of her mouth, his tender
touch, made Jasmine short of breath. "The one I started in the
hotel room?"

"On the best day of my life?" They sank into a hard,
demanding kiss that ended with Sarge yanking Jasmine closer
on the dresser, rolling in an intoxicating rhythm between her
thighs. "The day you came back to me? Yeah. That one."

Oh, and they had been working on *way* more than one
song. Since Sarge had brought music back into Jasmine's life,
she couldn't stop writing. Singing. More often than not, Sarge
joined her, encouraging her simply by adding his voice to
hers, turning her creations into duets. Sexy ones that fit the
Old News vibe. A few that would even make it onto the new
album. Some of Jasmine's best new memories of Los Angeles
were lying on their bedroom floor singing up at the ceiling
while Sarge strummed his guitar, ocean waves breaking down
below.

Jasmine's voice was thready when Sarge's skillful mouth
finally gave her the chance to answer. "We won't sing anything
if you don't go get on stage."

Sarge's blue eyes lit up. He knew he had her. There was
something else there, though. Additional mischief. "Is that a
yes?"

Leaping had become easier, so much easier, because she
knew they would always catch each other. Every time. "That's
a yes."

His smile fell away little by little, but those eyes remained focused on her. So focused. "I love you, Jasmine. But I dreamed about you so long, I'm still not sure I'm awake right now."

"You are." Heat pressed behind her eyelids. "I know because you woke me up, too. And I never want to go back to sleep."

He enfolded her in his arms and squeezed. "I'll see you out there, baby."

Sarge gave her a long look over his shoulder as he walked out of the dressing room. As soon as he was out of sight, Jasmine fell back against the wall, breathing deeply to get the hormones her boyfriend had unleashed back under control. The struggle was real. A corner of her mouth ticked up when she heard the crowd lose their minds over Sarge walking onstage…and then she heard the first few chords of "Girl in Blue."

*Dios,* the man knew how to make her heart pound.

Last week, Old News had gotten their upcoming tour schedule from the record label. Twenty-two countries over the course of a year once the new album was completed. Jasmine was loath to put her voice lessons on hold, but with the help of webcams, she could continue them from the road. She could still remember that afternoon when the schedule had been announced. Sarge had looked over at her in the meeting, obviously worried she might balk about accompanying the band on such an extensive tour. She'd seen his stubborn side rising to the surface and knew he wouldn't go without her. Informing Sarge—with a whisper in his ear—that she had no intention of being without him for any length of time had ended the way most of their conversations did. Back at home. With Sarge praying to God between Jasmine's thighs, in between licks.

James walked into the dressing room, bursting her naughty

thought bubble like a day-old balloon. "You coming?"

*Interesting choice of words.* Jasmine straightened. "Already?" She checked the wall clock. "They just walked out."

"You can't hear them chanting your name?"

Her heart slowed at the band manager's casually delivered question. Closing her eyes, she listened hard and heard it. The distant rumbling of her name. *Jasmine. Jasmine.* A hand lifted to circle her aching throat as she slid off the desk. "What am I supposed to do now?"

"Now?" James signaled that she should precede him to the stage. "You go out and sing. Later, we'll talk about the fact that the band already voted to make you the newest member. Which means…" He eyed the wall clock. "Technically, you're late for your first gig."

Jasmine's legs shook as she walked through the backstage area, past the roadies who patted her on the shoulders, and out onto the stage to deafening applause. Sarge met her halfway across the stage where a second microphone was already set up. The second he took her hand and they locked eyes, her legs stopped shaking.

They sang together. And they always would.

# Acknowledgments

Thank you Patrick and Mackenzie for loving me, continuing to believe in me, cheering for me, feeding me, and keeping me sane.

Thank you Heather Howland at Entangled Publishing for being a great, supportive editor, and loving tattooed men in beanies.

Thank you Margarita V. for inspiring the character of Jasmine! I appreciate you reading the rough draft and filling in the curse word blanks—it wouldn't have been right without them. And I still miss those walks to Starbucks.

Thank you Aquila Editing (aka Eagle) for beta reading *Crashed Out*. And loving Sarge's penchant for praying to Jasmine's lady parts.

Thank you Nelle OBrien for always being on messenger and being an all around fantastic lady. And for bullying me into being organized.

Thank you to Sara Eirew for taking the fabulous photograph on this cover. It's definitely my favorite cover to date. Such emotion and heat! Amazing.

Thank you Jillian Stein for being a huge, encouraging presence in my life and a most entertaining road trip companion.

Thank you to my Bailey's Babes, as always. Love you guys like FAS. ;)

# About the Author

New York Times and USA TODAY bestselling author Tessa Bailey lives in Brooklyn, New York, with her husband and young daughter. When she isn't writing or reading romance, she enjoys a good argument and thirty-minute recipes.

www.tessabailey.com
Join Bailey's Babes!

RAW REDEMPTION

BOILING POINT

OWNED BY FATE

EXPOSED BY FATE

DRIVEN BY FATE

*If you love sexy romance, one-click these steamy Brazen releases...*

## SCORING OFF THE FIELD
### a *WAGS* novel by Naima Simone

Football is Dominic Anderson's life. With his contract soon up for renewal, his focus needs to be on the game. But Tennyson—his dependable, logical best friend—is making that impossible with her mysterious new job and sudden interest in online dating. He doesn't do relationships. But the thought of another man touching her has him grasping at the chance for hot, no-strings sex that she offers. It's simple, uncomplicated...until it's not.

## TAKING A SHOT
### a Montana Wolfpack novel by Taryn Leigh Taylor

Hockey star Brett Sillinger's never been afraid of a little trouble. But when his personal life ends up in the tabloids, he knows his career is on thin ice. Luckily, a new team decides to take a chance on him. All he has to do is keep head in the game. But when Chelsea London, the owner's daughter walks in, looking for one night of nameless, no-strings passion, well, what's a guy to do?

## SAY YOU'RE MINE
### a *Shillings Agency* novel by Diane Alberts

Navy SEAL Steven Thomas has only ever been able to count on Lauren Brixton. She's been his best friend since grade school, and what they have is the *only* relationship he's managed not to ruin. Until one drunken night puts that all in jeopardy. Lauren knows Steven's not relationship material, so she does the only thing she can—she pretends she doesn't want him. But all's fair in love and war, and Steven's not about to lose the only person in his life who matters...

CPSIA information can be obtained
at www.ICGtesting.com
Printed in the USA
LVHW090851180122
708743LV00015BB/98